PRAISE FOR MJ JAMES

James's effective worldbuilding employs strong emotional and sensory descriptions ... often paralleling our society's own issues with neurodivergence, gender equality, economic disparity, and more.

THE BOOKLIFE PRIZE ON THE
IMMORTAL PART OF MYSELF

Good world-building and a storyline I was quickly hooked into.

GOODREADS REVIEWER ON IN-
BETWEEN

PHOENIX

THE EMBER TOWN SERIES
BOOK 2

MJ JAMES

*To all my fellow autistics,
you can do amazing things.*

Don't let anyone discount what you find amazing.

TRIGGER WARNING

Every day, autistic people hear how we are "wrong." We don't perform social rituals correctly, we don't make eye contact, and we doodle when we should be listening. There are millions of things we are told to "fix" about ourselves from childhood. It is no wonder that we can take that into ourselves. It is hard to find autistic joy when society tells us we can't be joyful about being autistic. Phoenix struggles with this as well. She may love who she is, but she has a lot of internalized ableism to work through, but she does work through it. However, as always, I will never have any hard feelings if you need to walk away from this story.

Phoenix Contains
Internalized Ableism
Externalized Ableism

ALSO BY MJ JAMES

In-Between

The Immortal Part of Myself

NeurodiVeRse

The Ember Town Series

Lucas

Phoenix

Birk

Phoenix's right pointer and middle fingers flicked wildly in front of her eye. The stimulation helped to calm her, and she allowed herself to indulge on the walk back from the vampire den to calm her nerves. As she approached her house, she forced her hand down to her side, but she was still restless. She allowed the fingers to tap against her thigh. As the heir to the pack, it would not be acceptable to have people see her act any weirder than she already did. It didn't matter that there was nothing wrong with providing herself with extra stimulation, or stimming. Phoenix knew this and believed it with all of her heart, but that didn't stop the looks from the rest of the pack who didn't understand. It didn't stop her father from thinking that she was not capable of being alpha. So, she minimized her movements and stopped to slow down her racing heart before she entered the pack house.

The pack house was located on the opposite side of town from the vampires. Where the vampires had a gated community with manicured lawns, the pack possessed a lot of open space with houses built up over the years as needed. They were set far apart, enough to keep werewolf ears from being able to hear through the insulation and across the distance to their neighbors. The houses had evolved as the families had changed, with little cubs being born and others going off to join different packs. In total, there were a hundred and four adult pack members at the moment. Her father, at age seventy-five, wasn't the oldest in the pack, but he was the alpha, a position that typically passed down from parent to child, when it was time. It would be years before Phoenix took the role, but there were responsibilities as the heir to the pack. It would be hers to defend and protect. Except, her autism left her fighting for her rights in the pack as much as fighting to defend it.

The main building was larger than the rest. It was the alpha's home but also a community space where the pack gathered. There were three stories; the top was set aside for her and her dad, even though that space was too large for just the two of them.

Phoenix had hoped that the house would be quiet when she arrived. While werewolves were not as set on sleeping during the night, the majority of the pack preferred it, as it was easier to interact with the human population. Phoenix was partial to the quiet of the night and felt the most restless while her father slept. Others in the pack felt the same way, and when Phoenix walked into the main floor of the house, she found a small gathering.

"Where have you been, fire girl?"

Phoenix turned and saw her cousin holding a beer and standing up while a group of young adult males sat around him. She made eye contact with him, refusing to answer, refusing to give him the upper hand. She was still the heir, at least for now.

1 … 2 … 3 … 4 … 5 … 6… She counted in her head as their eyes locked. Eye contact came naturally to the pack, with the less dominant pups, and non-alpha adults, breaking it off early. When Phoenix hadn't instinctively made eye contact as a child, she was seen as weak, lesser, and she'd had to learn to maintain her gaze. It hurt, almost a physical sensation, to remain locked onto someone's eyes, but she did it unblinkingly. *7 … 8 … 9 … 10 … 11…* Normal eye contact was about four seconds. It was less when a wolf looked at a dominant. Even high ranking as he was in the pack, her cousin should have looked away. *12 … 13 … 14 … 15 … 16 … 17 … 18 … 19 … 20 … 21 …* The pups were starting to shift as they sat. All were hyper-aware of the dominance game going on right in front of them, and no one was willing to show that they were acknowledging it. They fidgeted with their beer bottles or became very inter-ested in the carpeting. *22 … 23 … 24 …* The counting helped to deal with his eyes intently focused on her own. *25 … 26 … 27 …* He was testing her, pushing for her spot. He thought it was his, but she was still heir and he would learn his place. *28 … 29 … 30 …* It had been going on for too long. *31 …* She needed to act. *32 …* If he would not relent, then she would have to challenge him. *33 …* She started to open her mouth to call him out when his gaze dropped lazily to her chin. She had won, for now.

Slowly, the room began to wake up. A few pups started talking to each other, and eventually, her cousin began one of his stories which had everyone hanging off each word he spoke. Phoenix waited until the tempo of the room had returned to normal and then walked out of the living room to the kitchen. It was a large space, designed to feed the entire pack, with two ovens and an extra stovetop built into part of the island. The room could easily fit a group of busy adults cooking up a pack meal, and it often did. Now it stood empty and Phoenix took the time to center herself. The adrenaline of approaching the vampire horde had not left her. The relief at being given time to find Veronica and keep the council was short-lived. Now she had to convince her father of the same plan. But before that, she had to go back out to the pack and be seen. After that power play, she could not run off and hide in her room, even though that was all she wanted to do.

Phoenix opened the large fridge door and pulled out a bottle of beer. She hated the stuff and would normally have preferred anything else, but being in charge was as much about image as it was about her, and she had to think through every part of her public mask; none of it came naturally. The noise from the common room had picked up, and the pack had separated off to different tasks. She heard the crash of the balls on the pool table and the hum of the television as someone continually switched the channel.

Her headphones were sitting on the kitchen counter where she had left them. She wanted to slip them on, their noise cancellation specially calibrated to werewolf ears, helping to cut out some of the sounds that vibrated around her. Werewolves heard very well, but she seemed to be the only one who could not naturally filter out all the noise. There was always the hum of electricity and the thrum of water flowing, and on bad nights, like tonight, she could even hear the swish of cars as they drove by on the freeway a mile away.

Phoenix reached for her headphones, slipping them on

for a few seconds of peace before releasing a large sigh. She took the headphones off, picked the beer back up, and headed into the common room.

Jared, her cousin, was standing around the pool table with his two closest friends. He was tall, six and a half feet, with a broad frame. He had blond hair that hung to his shoulders in a light wave and a chiseled chin that screamed masculinity. He was exactly the person she would have picked to model on the front of one of those urban fantasy books that thought to romanticize the magical community. It was easy to see why her father was drawn to him. Maybe even Phoenix could have accepted him as alpha, if he wasn't so dense. But he was, and as heir, it was Phoenix's job to save the pack, even from itself. She had to step up and show her father why she needed to be officially recognized. It was past time. Her name day had come and gone. She had entered the official pack rank, but no official acknowledgment had come. That had been eleven years ago, on her sixteenth birthday. It had put the pack in an awkward position that also affected the rest of Ember's magical community.

But he hadn't appointed Jared yet, either. There was still a chance to show her father. She just needed to find and capture Veronica and convince him he could have faith in her.

Phoenix walked over to the arm of one of the couches and sat on it. Occasionally, she would raise her beer and take the smallest of sips. She didn't need to do anything. She just needed to be present. Her father had taught her that the mere presence of an alpha stabilized the pack. It was better that she had never really been one of them. They had never had to transition from seeing her as a playmate to a dominant. She had always been the alpha's weird daughter, but her place was here, guarding the pack, not like her cousin talking smack about the game.

Phoenix pulled herself out of her thoughts. It wasn't safe to be there tonight. She looked at the room, counting each wolf. There were only six, their presence seeming to take up so much more space than humans. Two sat in front of the large-screen television, finally having stopped on an old baseball game; the concept of rerun sports would forever baffle her. One lone wolf sat on a beanbag chair, playing a handheld video game. These were all wolves around her age, the ones that had grown up with her and Jared. Phoenix had been the only female in the group, causing a bigger divide every time she was challenged and won, whether from arm wrestling or the top score of a test. Each day, she had lost more of herself to come out on top because an alpha always had to be on top.

After a half hour, Phoenix started to get restless. She had plans to make, and she needed a way out of the room while saving face. So she was overjoyed when the last member of their cohort walked in. Ancel was a year younger than her and the only wolf that she truly called a friend.

"Having fun?" he asked as he came to a stop a few steps beside her, his eyes slightly downcast to acknowledge her status.

"Yes, it is a great party. Care to join?"

He looked around as if considering and then turned back. "I'd love to. Unfortunately, I have a problem and was wondering if you had a few moments to help me."

"Of course. Have fun, boys," she said in her best

nonchalant voice, the one she had practiced over and over. Phoenix led the way out of the room and out of the house. They kept walking until the voices began to dim. Finally, they reached a large oak tree, the spot that indicated it was safe for them to speak without being overheard.

"So, how did it go?" Ancel asked.

Phoenix looked to make sure that no one was around and then rubbed her hand against the bark of the tree. The rough texture soothed her in a way that being in a room surrounded by the pack did not. Ancel stood still, giving her the time she needed to compose herself. Finally, she let out a sigh and started talking.

"I made it to the house and the vampire leader, Elizabeth, let me in. Every vampire was there. It looked like they had been called back and were preparing for war. They all stopped and congregated in their big foyer while we talked. They were everywhere, still as statues, all over the stairs and ground, not even pretending to breathe."

"You made it out," Ancel said. "That must mean something."

"I have a week to catch Veronica and convince my father to step down from the council. If I do that, then they won't start a war."

"A week," Ancel said. He climbed up into the branches, facing the sky, as if waiting for the sunrise like they had done many times before.

"A week," Phoenix spoke softly, but she knew Ancel could hear her. "I have a week to convince my father, capture a vampire in bloodlust, and stop a war. Why did I think I could do this?"

She started to walk around the tree on a well-worn path. Her fingers flew back up to her face, flickering rapidly.

"Why did I think I could do this?" she said again.

"Then don't," Ancel said. "Stop now and let Jared have the pack. We can leave and find someone looking for strays, or we could go lone wolf."

"I can't do that." Phoenix stopped walking, her fingers frozen as she stared up at him in disbelief. "They would go to war. The pack couldn't survive a war with him as alpha. Think of all the humans that would be caught in the middle. We can't just abandon them."

Ancel jumped down and took her hands in his own, giving them a firm squeeze. "We won't. You can do this. I know that you can do this. You went and brokered a truce with the vampires. You did that while Jared was busy playing with his friends. You put your life on the line for the pack."

"I did do that," Phoenix said. "I walked into the heart of vampire territory." Her breath caught at the realization and her body started to tremble.

"Deep breaths." Ancel wrapped his arms around her firmly, giving her the pressure he knew she needed. They both slipped down to the ground while Phoenix attempted to catch her breath and control her trembling. Time stopped when she was in the middle of an attack, and when she started to return to herself, the sun was peeking above the horizon.

"It's okay," Ancel said. Phoenix realized he had been speaking soothing words to her the entire time.

"He will be up soon, if he isn't already," Phoenix said.

"You have time."

"I need to speak to him." Phoenix pushed on his arms, but without conviction.

"It will not do you any good until you are ready."

"What good will it do them to have an alpha who breaks into panic attacks?" Phoenix asked. She broke out from his arms then and stood up, using the sleeves of her shirt to try to clean off the tears that had stained her face. She could not face her father like this.

"Can you lead us or not?"

The question stopped Phoenix in her tracks. She turned back and looked at her friend. They had been inseparable since fifth grade when it became apparent that he was gay. The pack was more open with sexuality and gender than the witches, but they dealt much better with it when it was abstract rather than something that affected the pack. When the rest of the kids had stopped playing with him, Phoenix had built up her courage and said hello. They had been inseparable ever since. He had always believed in her.

"I can lead the pack. I have to lead the pack. I may be autistic, but when it matters, I am focused and engaged. It is only after that it hits me. My father thinks my autism is a liability to the pack, but it's not. I may be different, but those differences are what the pack needs right now."

"Then stop questioning yourself. It takes too much of your time and energy. You and I both know that you need to be the next alpha. We know that you are going to be amazing at it. Put all that energy into making everyone else realize it too instead of into convincing yourself repeatedly." Ancel walked away then, without her dismissal.

By the time Phoenix made it inside, the sun's rays had started the day. The party from the night before had been cleaned up, although Jared and his two goons were sitting at the kitchen table having breakfast with her father. She wanted to skirt past them, head up to her room, and get some sleep. Instead, she went over to the stove, scooped some eggs from the pan, and added a slice of buttered toast. Thinking better of it, she also added several sausage links. It was a smaller plate of food than the other wolves, but Phoenix had never had an enormous appetite.

Carefully, she took her plate to the table and stood behind Jared. He had dared to take the seat to the right of her father, and that had to be rectified. When Jared didn't move, Phoenix started to growl. It was low initially, just enough for him to know she was serious. When he still didn't move, she growled louder.

Jared looked at the alpha, who was staring intently at his food, letting the situation play out on its own. Jared turned and looked back at his food and continued to eat.

Phoenix could not let this pass. That was her seat and he

was telling her he was taking her position. If she let it pass, then she would be giving up the pack. There were so many rules and expectations. It was all exhausting.

With a sigh, she struck out and threw a low roundhouse kick to the chair legs. They broke just as easily as the plywood boards her father had used when teaching her martial arts. With the legs gone, the chair tilted back and fell to the ground, causing Jared to crash to the floor. Briar and Camron stood up as if to defend him, but with one glance from the alpha, they sat straight back down.

Phoenix pushed Jared's food out of the way, put down her plate, and prepared to fight. She was a stocky girl, but it was all muscle honed by years of training that had started when she was very young. She might have been eight when she'd spoken her first word, but she had been three when she'd thrown her first punch. Jared was large but had spent more time partying than applying himself. Phoenix had taken him in a fight before and knew she would have to do it again.

Jared started to get up, so Phoenix used the same move and kicked his feet out from under him. He fell back down to the ground.

"What the fuck," he said as he picked up speed and crawled away from the table before springing to his legs.

Phoenix watched him, knowing it would not be considered sporting if she didn't give him a chance to defend himself. However, once he was up, she struck quickly, moving in with a right and left to his stomach and then a hook kick that threw him off balance.

Jared growled as he charged her. Phoenix was able to block the blows before they landed. They had moved away from the table and skirted around the counters. She knew she had to do minimal damage to the kitchen while still keeping the upper hand. She wasn't sure Jared would display the same restraint. But when he grabbed the toaster oven from the counter while Phoenix dodged his blows, her father gave a loud grunt before returning his attention to his plate. Jared returned the toaster oven, and everything on the kitchen counters immediately became off-limits.

She needed to end this, and she needed to do it now, in such a way that she caused no humiliation but left no doubt about who won. Her mind circulated possibilities as she continued to evade and block. Jared was growing cocky, assuming he had her on the run, but it was more that she was trying to find the least embarrassing way to make him lose.

Finally, she had it, a solution so simple she knew her father would be disappointed that it had taken her so long. While Jared was coming at her, she sidestepped and punched her left hand right into his nose. It crunched, causing blood to rush down his face. First blood went to her and all he would have to do was shift to have his nose pop into place. As long as he did it soon, there would be no permanent damage.

She walked away from him, his blood still on her hand, and pushed the broken chair fragments out of the way as she pulled over a new seat. She sat down and took her first bite of the now-cold food, pretending she wasn't slightly out of breath. Briar and Camron sat tense at the table, not eating, but also not leaving.

"How was your night?" her father asked.

"That fucking pup cheated," Jared said. The blood was still flowing freely, distorting his words. "There is no way that moron could take me in a fight. She can't lead the pack. She can barely speak a sentence."

At times, being autistic came with an advantage; none of the frustration that swirled inside her was visible on her face. Phoenix started to stand up again, so very tired of always having to defend her position, but before she could, her father laid a hand on her arm and then rose from the table.

He wasn't as tall as Jared, two inches shorter, but his presence towered over the pup. Jared instinctively moved his gaze to the ground and scrunched up his shoulders.

"What do you have to say about my daughter?"

"Nothing, sir." The words came out like a squeak, without the arrogance he had possessed just seconds before.

"She sits in her space, inherited from birth and won with first blood. Before you question her abilities, you should remember that she has been trained by me. An alpha does not lead with insults. He leads by example, always putting the pack's needs before his own. You may sit on my left. But for now, you may go."

Briar and Cameron took the words as an excuse to leave. They were out the door almost before the sentence was finished. Jared kept his head bowed, but it didn't hide his grimace. Phoenix knew he wouldn't give up so easily, but he did saunter backward toward the door. When he closed it, he slammed it so hard that the house shook in its frame, but it had been built to withstand generations of were-wolves and held steady.

Phoenix focused on her food as her father returned to his breakfast. He had not named her his heir. That alone would give Jared even more permission to try out for her spot. The fight itself should have been enough for her to at least be awarded the title of heir spoken rather than assumed.

The alpha pushed his plate away and folded his hands on the table. He would leave at any moment. Now was her chance to speak.

"Father, I would like permission to head into Denver."

"Now is hardly the time to be taking a vacation." Disappointment laced his tone. "The council is dissolving, and the vampires are preparing for war. I need you here now more than ever. You are one of my most skilled fighters."

"There should be no war. The council doesn't need to end." Phoenix wished for the millionth time that she had his way with words so she could make him understand what was in her head.

"Explain."

It was one simple word, but it was enough of an invitation that hope flared in Phoenix.

"I visited the vampires."

He stood up then, his face full of rage, and possibly, concern. Other wolves could sense emotions at a glance or a sniff, but Phoenix was stuck guessing, cut off from senses that were considered necessary in her pack.

"What right did you have to approach them? You could have been killed."

Phoenix stood up as well, trying to school her posture so that she was not challenging her father but showing him her strength. "It is my right and responsibility as heir to this pack. It had to be done, and if they chose to fight, then I would give my life for the safety of these pups. That is what you taught me being alpha meant. Am I wrong?"

"You are not wrong." He sat back down, his body loose, as if giving in. Only Phoenix was allowed to see him like this, not on guard and not putting on a performance. "Why did you not speak to me first?"

"You would have denied me even though it was my role to fill. Either denounce me or name me, but this gap in your heir is hurting the pack, so I will play my role until you fill it with another. The vampires agreed to stand down for a week so that I could go and hunt Veronica for them. If I do, they will rejoin the council, as long as you step down as chair."

"They expect you to clean up their mess and then hand over control to those cold-blooded monsters?"

Phoenix reached out slowly to ensure he knew her intent, and took his hand in his own. "They are not monsters any more than we are. We are allies, and you have overstayed your time as head of the council. The rules dictate that you stand down, and you did not. You may refuse to name me heir, but I will do what I need to for the good of the pack."

He looked at her, not as her alpha, but as her father, and she tried to return his gaze through the discomfort. She was so tired of losing herself for the good of others, but that is what leaders did. If only her father could see that.

"One week," he said at last.

Phoenix nodded.

"You can do it?"

"I will take Ancel with me. We will capture her together. There is no other choice."

"You may go, but you will need more than just that young pup at your side. Let me think about it. Go sleep, and when you wake, we can prepare."

"I plan to leave this afternoon."

He nodded absently, his focus already moving on to

plans. Phoenix picked up both their plates and rinsed them. One of the pack would be by later to fully clean up, but she tried to leave as little for them to do as possible. Then she headed upstairs to her room. He might not have acknowledged her status, but he had at least given her permission to defend the pack. Yet the anxiety still wouldn't leave her.

Phoenix sent Ancel a text and set her phone alarm. She needed to sleep since she had been awake for twenty-four hours. There was no telling what they would face when they made it to Denver, but the anxiety wouldn't leave her alone enough to settle down. She refocused her restless energy into packing. Phoenix had not traveled all that much. Her father had taken her on a few trips to meet with other packs, but given the choice, she would choose to stay in Ember surrounded by everything that she knew.

Denver only lay about a hundred miles northeast of their town, but it seemed like a world away. Phoenix had not visited since she had been a child and had become so overwhelmed with the noise that she had been sent home early. Now, she needed to protect her pack, and she did not have the luxury of hiding in her room, as much as she wanted to.

Her room was the one place that was truly hers. Even Ancel did not come up to the third floor of the alpha's house. Her walls had been soundproofed, which helped to soften the noise that was a constant thrum around her.

Double-layered blackout curtains covered the windows, not allowing in the sun unless she opened them. Her bed was covered in soft purple blankets and softer stuffed animals. If anyone in the pack had seen it, they would have accused her of being a child, but her father had taught her that even an alpha needed a place to recharge.

Phoenix studied the clothes thrown haphazardly in her closet and tried to determine what she would need to pack. Normally, she didn't think much about clothing. She put a few pairs of jeans in a duffle bag and threw in some T-shirts. After some thought, she added her spare pair of headphones, some earplugs, and a textured ball that fit in the palm of her hand. There were more sensory tools that she had picked up over the years, but they all stayed safely in her room. An alpha didn't show weakness.

With that done, there was nothing else to do but sleep. She lay down on her bed, allowing her animals to surround her, and threw on her weighted blanket, especially made to provide werewolf amounts of pressure. Usually, it was enough to help her fall instantly asleep, but this morning, her mind wouldn't shut off. Phoenix knew what she needed to do. She had to stop Veronica, stop the war, and keep the council alive. It was all so simple, but how to accomplish any of it eluded her.

She had gone to school with vampire kin, humans that were susceptible to being turned. Some students had even taken pleasure in this knowledge, playing vampires with ceramic teeth and dark clothes. They had stayed far away from the pack. All Phoenix knew about vampires was what her father had taught her, and as open-minded as he professed to be, it was obvious to her that he had his own prejudice against the creatures of the night.

Phoenix had insisted on attending council meetings since she had turned sixteen. Ember was a nexus, a place where magical energy met, and a natural attraction to magical beings. It was also one of the few such towns that had managed to create a place where multiple species lived in harmony. That was thanks to the council. Every major species had a seat, and every magical being had a vote. She had listened as the vampires had talked about being hunted and wanting a better life. It was what her people wanted as well. She saw the pains they went to in order to ensure that their life did not endanger humans, and she respected them for their choices.

Her father called them lawless, but Phoenix knew they just followed their own set of rules, ones stemming from their own history and traditions. It didn't make them wrong, or less than, just different. They could learn from each other; they had already learned from each other.

Phoenix's determination to maintain peace was unwavering. As alpha, she would make sure to continue the relationships between the magical community. Now, she just had to keep the peace long enough. That meant stopping Veronica. Phoenix didn't begrudge the vampires that one of their own had gone rogue. After all, she had to deal with Jared on a regular basis, and she didn't want all werewolves judged on his actions or even the stubbornness of her father. A new era was starting, and Phoenix needed to help her people through it.

At some point, she must have drifted off to sleep because the next thing she knew, her alarm clock was going off, letting her know that it was eleven a.m. and that it was time to get ready to go.

When Phoenix entered the living room, Ancel was already there, waiting. He had carry-on-size luggage and a full backpack at his feet. Phoenix looked at her deflated duffle bag and rethought whether she had packed enough.

"I like to be prepared," Ancel said.

It took Phoenix a second to realize that he was defensive. He must have read her glance as her thinking he had overpacked. Phoenix opened her mouth to tell him her concerns, but her father entered the room before she could get the words out.

"We are about to head out," Phoenix said. The anxiety started to creep in. He had already agreed but could easily change his mind, and Phoenix had no alternative plan.

"Where is Jared?"

Phoenix looked at Ancel, confused by why she was required to know where the wolf was and hoping he somehow knew. But Ancel just shrugged, and Phoenix turned her attention back to her father. "I don't know."

"Well, you better find out."

"Why do I need to know where he is?"

"I told you that you needed a third person to go. Ancel is a good pup, but the boy doesn't know how to throw a punch. You need someone who can watch your back."

Phoenix ran through his words and focused on the ones she thought were the most important. "Ancel is a much better fighter than Jared. I think I showed you this morning how horrible of a fighter Jared is."

"You really should have ended the fight faster. You need to think quicker in high-stress situations."

Phoenix had known the critique was coming, but it didn't lessen the sting. She should have come up with the solution earlier. An alpha must always be one step ahead to do what is best for her pack. She took a deep breath, letting it settle before answering. "Yes, sir." Her response was devoid of any sign of emotion. Then she turned to Ancel. "Are you ready?" She readjusted her bag on her shoulder and headed to the kitchen door.

When Phoenix didn't hear Ancel's footsteps behind her, she stopped and turned around. He was still sitting on the couch, nervously playing with the zipper on his backpack. She was missing something. Phoenix reviewed the conversation in her head, trying to understand his hesitation.

"Yes, sir. I will make sure not to make the same mistake in our hunt for Veronica," Phoenix said. "I think it is best for us to go now. We want to make it to the city before night."

Her father looked at her with disappointment. It was an expression that she had seen often enough in her childhood. She just didn't understand *how* she was letting him down.

"We need to bring Jared," Ancel said.

Phoenix looked at her father in surprise. "Didn't we

already establish that he was a horrible fighter and would not be helpful? We still have to bring him?"

"Yes." The response was firm, and the tone brokered no question.

Phoenix didn't understand why she was not enough for her father. Maybe declaring her heir at sixteen would not have been accepted by the pack. She had barely spoken, and flinched anytime someone tried to talk to her. She had hummed incessantly and twirled around, watching the sky spin far above. But she had worked so hard the last eleven years to learn how to hide this part of herself. Being alpha meant giving yourself to the pack. She had given them everything, but her father still found ways to tell her it was not enough. Jared just existed, and that seemed to be more than enough. Phoenix and Ancel had beaten him in every fight, both on the mat and behind the school, since they were in sixth grade. Jared spent less time at meetings and more time with his buddies, causing trouble or doing whatever, and yet he was being sent to babysit them.

"Isn't there someone else you can send with us?" Phoenix asked.

"It's important he joins you. He needs to show the pack he has what it takes to protect them, and this is the perfect opportunity for that. This will be a good experience for him. I know you are more aware of what has been happening with this situation, so I am counting on you to keep him informed and help advise him along the way. This is important. We need this to keep us from war."

And there it was. Everything Phoenix had worked for had been ripped away and explained back to her. She knew her father loved her, but he also did not think she could lead the pack. It hurt, but what mattered most was taking care of the pack. Phoenix would do everything in her power to ensure the pack stayed safe, even if it meant giving Jared credit for what she and Ancel were about to do, because she knew this was beyond Jared's capabilities. Phoenix wasn't even sure how the two of them would accomplish it.

"Yes, sir," Phoenix said. Her voice held all her hurt and disbelief, but her father didn't hear any of it.

"One last thing," he said. "Cancel whatever reservations you made. There is a lone wolf in the city. He is an old friend of mine, and he agreed to let you stay at his place. He was very concerned to hear a vampire was encroaching on his territory and was more than willing to help join in the fight. I'll text you his address and phone number."

Phoenix nodded and headed toward the exit. This time, Ancel raced after her. They didn't speak as they walked to his car and threw their bags in the trunk. It wasn't until they were already on the road that he turned to her. "You never had reservations made, did you?"

Phoenix glanced down at her hands, refusing to give him an answer, but he knew her well enough to recognize it was answer enough. He let out a chuckle. "Alright, let's go find where Jared is hiding."

But Phoenix didn't find the humor in the situation. If she had forgotten that they would need a place to sleep, what else had she forgotten?

They sat on the side of the road with the engine running. Ancel flipped through music on his phone while Phoenix slumped in her seat. Jared wasn't at his house or either of his buddy's houses.

"We tried our best. I'm sure my father would understand if we didn't bring him. It's not like we can wait all night."

Ancel just gave her a look before turning back to his phone.

"Fine. He would lose his mind, but how can he think Jared is fit to be alpha if he can't even show up?"

Phoenix picked up her phone and dialed Jared's number again. It rang until transferring her once more to his voicemail. She hung up before leaving another message.

"If I can't find the stupid pup, then I'm not fit to be alpha. Where do a bunch of overgrown boys go to hang out?"

"Do you think they are at the bar?"

"Great idea," Phoenix said.

With a new destination to try, they headed off to

Rocko's. The bar had been a favorite place of theirs back when they had both turned twenty-one. Ancel had discovered it first, a way to hook up with humans visiting for business or a night on the town without having to worry about who he was. On the quiet nights, Phoenix had occasionally tagged along. There was something safe about the space, and no one told her to take off her earphones or gave her a hard time about her dancing. Everyone was respectful; Rocko wouldn't accept anything less.

Then, a few years ago, Jared found the bar, and he and his friends took it over. Nothing was stopping Ancel and Phoenix from visiting it, and they still did on occasion when they knew Jared wouldn't be around. But they had to be careful. Rocko didn't allow dominance fights, and Jared took every opportunity to treat Phoenix as if he were in charge.

When werewolves gathered, it was expected they would hang out together, and anytime Ancel had tried to hook up with Jared's friends around, they had found subtle ways to stop it from happening. Rocko's was as much a queer bar as a magical one, and outright discrimination would not be tolerated. But Jared had always found ways to let Ancel know he didn't approve of him.

When they stepped inside the bar, Phoenix was surprised at how much had changed since the last time she had visited a month ago. It wasn't in the decoration as much as in the atmosphere. There was a sense of tension in the air so thick she could smell it. The bar was less than a quarter full, and even the humans were sequestered to their spots, focusing on their drinks.

Behind the bar was a young selkie instead of the human who had worked there before. Phoenix gave him a nod of acknowledgment to show the proper respect. It was Rocko's territory, but the selkie was acting as his representative, and it would not be proper to let that go unrecognized.

After that formality was done, Phoenix looked around the bar properly.

Mika, the witch, was sitting at her usual table. She was here so much that she might as well have her name carved into the place. When the witch caught her looking, Phoenix had no choice but to hold her gaze until Mika gave a slight nod and returned to her beer. Thankfully, it was just long enough to show that she wasn't a pushover but not long enough to cause Phoenix the pain she felt with eye contact, yet another reason she wasn't wolf enough.

Jared was with four other pack members. They were the liveliest group in the place, as if they were so clueless as to be unable to read the room. Phoenix did not have a lot of respect for Jared, but even she knew he was better than that. He was putting on a show, making her chase him down and prostrate herself to start the mission.

Phoenix hated dominance games passionately, and even though she was not naturally gifted at them, she had been studying them since childhood. So, she did what needed to be done. She went to the opposite corner of the bar, pulled out a chair, and joined the pixies. She split her attention between giving them the appropriate greeting, in as close as she could to their high-pitched language that was beyond the normal human audio range, and watching Ancel, who had gone to the bar and ordered two bottles of beer. Phoenix hated beer, but this was all about the show, and it was a perfect prop for what would go down. He brought the bottles, put them both in front of Phoenix, waited until she took her pick, and had a healthy chug before he picked up his own. Then he pulled up his chair, positioning it slightly back from Phoenix, signifying her dominance.

The pixies were an interesting group. They were all socially one gender, even if not biologically so. Pixies had a very skittish society, and the hive in Ember was the only one known to have settled in a city. They were considered diplomats of their kind, and when it came time to translate their culture, it was decided that, collectively, they would present as female, as it was the most comfortable for their natural expression.

Anyone who interacted with them was also treated as female. Most men tended to stay far away from them, but Phoenix and Ancel had become friends with the hive over the years. They were among the few people who could tell them apart by both look and smell; the differences were minor.

There was a group of four in the bar, although they moved around so much, it felt like there were more. The group had picked up on Phoenix's behavior and flittered in concern. Phoenix had communicated to them the best she could that there was a situation in her hive that she was trying to take care of. They acknowledged and asked how they could best support her. When Phoenix asked for time in their company, they happily agreed.

It had been over a month since she had last been in to catch up, and the pixies showered her with questions. They seemed highly concerned about the missing human bartender, Lucas, and did not understand what had caused his disappearance. They were creatures of habit, something Phoenix could intensely relate to. She explained that he could no longer work behind the bar because he had been turned into a vampire by Veronica. His turning had trig-gered Veronica's bloodlust and was the reason Phoenix needed to go and hunt her before the council disbanded and the magical communities went to war.

Phoenix only half listened to the conversation. Even as she tried to present herself as if she were ignoring Jared's existence, she was still aware of him behind her. But as the pixies continued to talk, it became easier to get lost in their stories.

Even so, she was aware when Jared stood up and pounded his fist on his table, screaming at one of the pups. A businessman at a nearby table suddenly decided his lunchtime was over. He left his half-eaten food behind before heading back to whatever corporate hellscape he had come from. Even the selkie slinked off from behind the bar back to the kitchen, probably going to warn Rocko.

As much as Phoenix needed to prove dominance, she did not want to cause a scene. So, she thanked the pixies for their time and agreed to visit them as soon as possible. After, she walked out of the bar with Ancel trailing behind her like a puppy.

The area outside the bar was bustling with activity. The hotels were only a few blocks away, and the charming downtown area attracted the few tourists the city acquired. Mostly, they were families of business people brought into the town to interact with the interests of the various magical communities, not that they knew this. It made for an awkward place for a pack brawl.

"We could make him go back to the house," Ancel said.

"By the time we arrived, he would have twisted it around. It needs to happen now, in front of his pack. I need to remind them who I am."

"The alley?"

Phoenix looked at the side of the bar. It was mostly empty, with just a few trash cans and stairs leading up to a second-floor door. If things went well, it would work, and if things didn't go well, Rocko would be sending them all home with their tails between their legs.

Jared stormed out of the bar, flinging the door open and stomping out a trail of anger so thick that Phoenix was sure even the humans could smell it. She made sure not to give any indication that she noticed him and then slipped down the side of the building, hoping Ancel would do his part to stay away.

"Looks like you got yourself trapped," Jared said as he followed her.

Phoenix stopped. She crossed her arms, holding her body still but showing she was in charge of the situation. She stood unspeaking, unwilling for him to gain the upper hand. She knew it was a risk. If he decided to attack, she would have to take him on and win. But she hoped he was at least smart enough to know that it wasn't a fight he *could* win.

"I don't know what you are playing at, coming to my spot and not acknowledging my presence and then going and hanging out with those pixie freaks instead of the pack."

Phoenix allowed her eyebrows to rise slightly, making sure it didn't show surprise but just a hint of disbelief that he could believe his own statement. She could picture what it looked like from all the hours she had spent in the mirror practicing the correct way to make it.

"You know I am lined up to be the heir. It is all but a done thing. Your father just needs to formally announce it."

That was the line on which she needed to make her opening. She had to move carefully now, allowing her to regain the upper hand.

"But he has not announced it yet, and until he does, I am still the heir, with all the rights and responsibilities thereof. You were due at the house an hour ago. The alpha ordered you, and instead of fulfilling your responsibilities to the pack, you decided to go off day drinking with your buddies." There was nothing wrong with the term "buddies," not precisely, but it minimized his control over them, putting them as his equals and letting them know that he was not their leader. Subtle messaging like that mattered to the wolves, and Phoenix had to remember to include it when she spoke.

"Like you could leave without me. You need me. No one will follow you."

It was the same line he had used since elementary school, and unlike when her father said it, it had lost all power over her. Phoenix knew that he was not an effective leader. She knew that he would not make a good alpha. He would lead the pack to ruin, which was why she had to step up.

"Right now, you have two choices. Choice number one is to get your ass in the car so that we can drive to Denver and stop a war. Choice number two is to walk over to the Ranch and tell them that you are the new heir to the pack and will be taking over the agreement I made with them last night."

The disbelief on his face was evident, but Phoenix stood there unmoving, her face impassive, letting him know she was serious. He stood watching her, waiting for her to break and take it back, giving him an easy opening. So she stood still, allowing her face to remain in her naturally unreadable expression. Phoenix could tell the moment he realized he was pinned into a corner; the raw scent of fear wafted off of him. It wasn't a lot, but it was enough for her to pick up on, which meant his friends at the entrance to the alley could smell it as well.

He stood staring her down, trying to save face, and she let him. Everyone here knew she had won, but rubbing his face in it would have been bad form. It would make her no better than he was.

Finally, he turned and walked out of the alley as if he were still in charge. "Come on. We are going to be late," he said.

But the shift was evident. His pack was no longer his own. They showed deference to Phoenix as she walked out — subtle nods, moving out of her way, falling behind her, acknowledging that she was their alpha. She let Jared walk off the length of a building before she asserted control again. "The car is this way." Then she strode off without looking back.

Ancel was right at her heels, showing both deference and support. When they reached the car, he opened the passenger door for her, as a matter of respect, before he went and took his place in the driver's seat. Phoenix had her driver's license. She'd passed the test and practiced enough that, given the need, she could take control of the wheel, but it wasn't something she enjoyed or was particularly good at. In this situation, it came in handy because it left Jared with no place to go except the back seat, a position that, under a different situation, Ancel would have had to take. She heard his growl through the window as he realized. Phoenix kept her attention forward, but she watched him out of the side mirror. He turned and looked at the wolves, who all stood around, observing the situation. His prolonging it was making this worse for himself. Finally, he relented, opening the door and sliding into the back seat. He nearly took off the car door when he slammed it close.

"You know, it wouldn't hurt to close things nicely," she said. It was such a small barb, but no one was around, and she enjoyed the opportunity to say it without him being able to start a pack war.

"Let's go and get this over with," he said.

Phoenix glanced around, wondering if he had magically come up with a bag to take, and then shrugged. He could figure it out on his own; they had wasted enough time on him.

"Let's go," Phoenix said.

On her cue, Ancel started the car and drove out of the lot, the wolves still watching.

The drive to the city took them through the backroads of the Rocky Mountains. It was not an exceptionally long drive, just around three hours, but the tension in the car was unbearable. Phoenix was glad that Ancel was at the wheel. She had enough anxiety just seeing the drop-off cliffs without being responsible for them not falling off. However, Jared had the opposite reaction. His need to control everything left him growling in the back seat for most of the ride. A few times, Phoenix had to turn around and growl at Jared herself to get him to leave well enough alone. However, the satisfaction of him naturally responding to her was intense, even if she kept that to herself so she didn't start an alpha war in the middle of the car.

By the time they made it to Denver, it was later than she wanted, although still a few hours before nighttime hit. Veronica was sure to be holed up somewhere, escaping the sun, giving them time to find their accommodations. The directions to the lone wolf's house led them to Lakewood, a city outside of Denver. He had set up on the west side of the city, allowing access for him to still escape into the woods.

The house wasn't large; it was more of a modern log cabin with a gravel driveway set back from the main road. Trees had been planted to obscure the entrance, and even with GPS, they almost missed it.

Phoenix wasn't used to being in another wolf's territory. When she had been brought to meet with other packs, it had always been on neutral territory, far from where anyone called home. Here, it smelled wrong. This is what it would mean for her if she lost her pack, but not completely. Phoenix knew if she left, Ancel would go with her. They would start their own pack, just the two of them and whoever Ancel mated with. The solo wolf's territory felt lonely, and Phoenix could not help but wonder who would choose such a life.

She didn't have to wait long to find out. Before the car finished pulling next to the pickup truck, a man exited the house. He wasn't tall by wolf standards, at just short of six feet. His slim, almost nerdy build was accentuated by the thin-rimmed, black-framed glasses that sat on his dark-skinned face. There were disabled wolves, and occasionally, there was damage that could not be shifted enough to fix. There was a wolf in their pack who regularly used a wheel-chair for mobility after a bear attack in her youth. And even shifting would not impact genetics or chromosomes. But it was rare that a wolf needed glasses. Unless there was irreparable neurological damage, the eyes would fix them-selves when you next shifted. This meant this wolf either didn't shift — and the scent of his property told Phoenix that was not the case — or he was wearing them for show.

Usually only the strongest of wolves downplayed who they were. She would need to be careful around him.

Jared didn't seem to have the same concern. He walked right up to the man, dominating over him, expecting him to bow down and give him respect. Except that was all wrong; they were on his territory as guests, not to take it over. Phoenix rushed out of the car, her arm tangling in the seatbelt as she tried to hurry out before Jared got himself killed. She tripped on the dirt road as she extricated herself from the car, but caught herself before making too much of an embarrassing scene.

"Thank you for inviting us to your home," Phoenix said.

The man sidestepped Jared, slipping around him like he was nothing before going to Phoenix. Phoenix was in awe of his response. It was on his territory, so he could have knocked down the wolf without any repercussions. However, doing so would have made Phoenix look bad. He had just declared his support for Phoenix, and she had done nothing to deserve it.

She inclined her head slightly, giving him respect without conceding dominance. He wasn't an alpha; some lone wolves were, and others were not. He just seemed to exist in a state all his own.

"My name is Einer. Welcome to my home. Your father mentioned you were here to hunt a vampire."

"Yes, one of the local vampire pack has gone rogue in Denver. Things are tense, and I have volunteered our own pack to help track her down."

"I am at your disposal. The last thing we need is a vampire in the city. We like to keep things quiet around here, mind our own business."

"We? I thought you were by yourself?"

"Yes, I'm a lone wolf, but a pack resides on the other side of town."

"Denver has a pack? Surely, my father would have told me about them."

"It's a second son and his wife. They have two small kids, so I told them I would handle the hunt if they protected their young ones."

A second son — it was what Phoenix was about to be if she didn't manage to get Jared under control before her father adopted him as heir. A second son, or child, of an alpha was often kicked out of the pack either for trying to take it over or for concern that they would eventually try to take over.

"You seem close. Are you not pack?" Phoenix knew it was a rude question as soon as it left her mouth. It was another moment of her speaking without thinking, wanting to know without needing to know. However, Einer didn't seem concerned with her question.

"I don't enjoy people all that much. We actually have a lot in common, although I am a bit concerned that your father views my behavior as the norm. Come on in. The house is yours to use, except for my room."

Einer turned and walked away, abruptly ending the conversation. It was something Phoenix would have done on a day when she didn't have the energy to pretend with all the social cues. It made her wonder what exactly he meant by having a lot in common. The wolf was her father's age and lived all alone.

Phoenix turned to Ancel, who had waited in the driver's seat in case they needed to make a fast exit, and let him know that all was good. Ancel picked up Phoenix's bag. She nearly protested, but Jared's behavior told her she needed to be treated like an alpha now more than ever.

The inside of the house wasn't big enough for four werewolves, especially when two were vying for alpha and a third held the territory. The front door opened into a living room with a large couch, a TV, a coffee table, and not much else. Ancel put their bags on the sofa and sat on the edge of it, as far out of the way as possible. Einer had disappeared, and that was just fine with Phoenix. It gave her some time to take the lay of the land, or it would have if Jared hadn't burst in the door after them and decided to try and take charge again.

He walked past the living room into a doorway that, judging from the scents, was probably the kitchen. Phoenix started counting in her head but didn't get past two before he walked back out again. Next, he stormed down the hallway connected to the living room. Phoenix moved slightly so she could see down the hall. It was just a row of shut doors. Jared began to pace up and down along it. Wolves did not go into each other's territory without permission. Einer had given them permission for the house but not the bedroom, and with the doors shut, there was no way of knowing which of the doors was for the bedroom, especially since the entire house smelled only of Einer. There hadn't been another werewolf in the home for quite some time.

Phoenix paced around the living room, taking it all in. There were only three doors in the hallway, which meant there were probably only two bedrooms and one bathroom. The living space would have to double as dorms as well as a command center. The couch was L-shaped; it could sleep two, but Jared wouldn't share, which meant Jared would get the couch, aside from when the pack needed it. Phoenix couldn't bring Ancel into the room with her. It was too intimate for someone who wasn't mated. So much time was wasted on politics when they should be focused on getting ready for the hunt.

Ancel was currently crouching on the ground between the end of the couch and the wall. There was a fairly large gap that contained only a potted plant and a magazine holder. Phoenix picked them up, relocating them, and threw a blanket down on the ground. It sucked that her friend couldn't have a better place, but Ancel seemed to be calmer now that he had his own assigned territory.

Next, Phoenix turned on the TV to the local news station. If anything out of the ordinary happened, they would want to know immediately. She was watching the news when Einer came out of his room. Jared tried to use it as the opportunity to open one of the other doors, claiming dominance, but Einer reached the doors first, put his hand on the doorknob, and called out for Phoenix. She walked toward him.

"I forgot to show you to your room." He made eye contact with Phoenix when she stepped into the small guest room. Ancel entered right behind her, dropping her bag on the twin-sized bed and moving out of the room again. She should have done it on her own, so he didn't have to enter her space, but she appreciated his foresight. Once the room was claimed as hers, Jared's only choice would be to start a fight or slink away. Thankfully, he chose to slink away.

Phoenix was happy to find out that the guest bedroom was soundproofed, just like her bedroom. The sound had been closing in on her from the drive and even in the small house. They might not be close enough to the next neighbor to hear them, but a house had so many overwhelming noises, from the electricity buzzing through the cords to the water flowing through pipes. And whoever said nature was quiet hadn't spent any time in it. Phoenix hadn't realized how much stress the sensory input was putting her through until she was finally away from it. She closed the door completely and sunk onto a soft, silky bedspread. She ran her hands over the texture while she closed her eyes and focused on breathing. The tension began to melt off her body. It was only a reprieve, but a welcome one. At least now she knew that whatever she had in common with the lone wolf, sensory overload was one of them. It had to be if he put this much attention into a barely-used guest bedroom.

By the time Phoenix walked back out of the room, Jared had centered himself in the middle of the large side of the couch, with his legs spread as far as possible. Einer ignored the display of dominance in his home and was busy in the kitchen making them all drinks.

"Now that we are here, it is time to make a plan," Phoenix said.

"Do you have a way of taking out a vampire?" Einer

asked as he carried four glasses carefully cupped in both hands.

Phoenix sniffed the drink and was glad it was just water. Then, she took a sip to show her appreciation for his hospitality before she continued.

"Things have moved fast, so we aren't exactly sure what the plan is. I think the first thing to do is make sure that Veronica has even headed this way. Once we have confirmation and better understand the situation, we can plan our move."

"We shouldn't wait," Jared said. "We need to make our move now."

"What would you suggest we do?" Phoenix asked.

"We could draw her out," Ancel said.

"No." Jared stood up as he talked and stopped beside Phoenix. "We need to go to her. "

"How do you suggest we do that if we don't know where she is?" Einer asked.

"She is a bloodsucker. Of course, we know where she will be. She will be out in the clubs trying to find her prey."

"Except Veronica's plan isn't to blend in. She wants to stand out, so I don't think she will be at a club," Phoenix said. "She will have to go somewhere she will be out of place but still get noticed at night. Einer, do you know where someplace like that would be?"

"I don't get out that much."

"This is ridiculous," Jared said. "While you are all here arguing, I could have already found her. I'm going to the clubs."

"Fine, but if you see her, make sure to text us before you confront her." But Jared had left the house before Phoenix had even finished speaking.

"What happens if he does find her?" Ancel asked.

"It doesn't make sense that she would be in the most obvious place and the place least likely to cause chaos if she unleashed her fangs. But if he does find her, then he will either neutralize her, which is the best-case scenario, or she will know that we are here. Either way, we still need to move forward I need to go out and understand the situation better."

"That isn't a good idea," Einer said.

"Why not?" Phoenix asked.

"This isn't like the small town. The sounds of city life, even at night, are overwhelming. You should send the pup to scout things out."

Phoenix looked at Ancel. He would go if she asked, but an alpha shouldn't ask someone to do a task she should be able to do. This was her job, and if she were going to lead the pack, she would have to figure out how to manage it.

"We should split up. You two can go out looking, and I can go separately. That way, we can cover double the territory. Just don't engage if you find her."

But Einer was disappearing into the kitchen, a barely audible murmur on his lips. "Nope, no way, not going to happen."

Phoenix let out a deep sigh and turned toward Ancel. "Will you stay here and keep an eye on Einer? I'll let you know if I find anything." And she turned and walked out the door.

Phoenix decided to take Ancel's car. There was no guarantee that Veronica would be heading into the main part of the city. Still, it seemed a more dramatic option than revealing herself in Littleton, Colorado, even if you couldn't tell the border between one end of the city and the start of the other.

She sat in the driver's seat, putting her hands on the steering wheel and familiarizing herself with the car. It had been a few years since she had last sat behind the wheel. As the daughter of the alpha, she used one of the pack cars on rare occasions, but this was the car she had learned to drive. Ancel had taught her. He was the only one who didn't see her differences as weaknesses. Phoenix didn't either, but it was hard to embrace her differences when the rest of the pack continued to use them against her.

Ancel appeared out the window, and Phoenix went to roll it down before realizing she couldn't because she didn't have the keys. Instead, she was forced to open the door, looking at him sheepishly, something she was aware an alpha should never do.

"Thought you might need these." He held out the keys to her.

"You can come if you want," Phoenix said.

"No, go do your thing. I'll stay here with the lone wolf and see if I can get more information from him. It's best to play all the angles."

Phoenix took the keys gratefully and started up the engine. She waited for Ancel to step back and then put the car in reverse, turning in the large space in front of the house so she could pull out easily to the road.

The drive into the city was down a highway. Lighting from houses framed the street, causing more of an issue than Phoenix expected, having only driven in her small town of Ember. The light caused flashes of starbursts, trying to distract her from the road. Whenever a car passed, their lights were extraordinarily bright, dazzling Phoenix's vision for a few seconds. There were more people on the road than she had expected, and while she knew that as an alpha, simply driving down the road should not be a problem, it didn't stop the headache from forming or the tension wrapping around her body.

If she were going to lead her pack, then she would need to be able to handle situations like this, so she stuffed the anxiety that was threatening to overwhelm her deep down into her bones and ignored the pain that coursed through her with each light she passed, and continued driving.

It took about thirty minutes for her to reach the area marked as downtown on her phone map. Phoenix pulled into the first empty spot on the side of the road, deciding it was best to do more surveillance on foot. She sat in the car, her fingers still clutching the steering wheel, and closed her eyes, trying to dismiss the phantom light that haunted her.

She waited until she could no longer hear her heart pounding against her chest before she opened her eyes, unclasped her seatbelt, and opened the car door.

The sky was dark, the moon hidden behind buildings, but neon and fluorescent lights lit the streets. Noise began to assault her as soon as she opened the car door. There were people everywhere, more people than Phoenix had ever seen together in her town. They wandered in pairs or small groups toward businesses. They sat on restaurant patios talking to each other. The conversations flooded Phoenix, all the words hitting her at once, unable to make out any of them.

Music spilled out when doors were opened or as cars drove past. The lights hummed at their own pace, some consistently and others in a thrumming pattern, causing a jumble of sound. The scent of unwashed bodies and unclean toilets drifted from the sewers and alleys, mixing unpleasantly with the smell of fried food drifting from a restaurant kitchen.

No wonder wolves don't live in big cities, Phoenix thought. Even wolves without Phoenix's extra sensitivity would have difficulty in a crowded city such as LA or New York. Denver was not nearly as big, but it was so much louder than anything Phoenix had ever heard.

She turned back in the car, going to reach for her head-phones, to at least cancel out some of the noise, but they weren't there. In her haste, she must have left them back at Einer's house.

With a sigh, she emerged fully from the car, checking to make sure she had the keys before locking it up. Now, she had to figure out where to start.

Phoenix walked past a bus stop, something she had only

seen in movies. There was a full poster advertisement of the Red Rocks Amphitheater advertising The Zombiez' concert. They were a rock band that Ancel loved to listen to, although Phoenix didn't understand the appeal of the scratching sounds. He had talked about going but knew Phoenix would never be able to handle the noise. It was tomorrow night, and she wondered if there were tickets left. Maybe she could get a pair and surprise her friend. Jared would go with him if she played it right. She looked at the tagline for the event, "Come party with the dead," and rolled her eyes. It was so dramatic, even if the background was beautiful. However, she preferred nature to be as far away from people as possible, not turned into an amphitheater attracting large crowds.

Phoenix continued following the noise, hoping that the louder it was, the more likely she would be to find Veronica. She walked through a courtyard that was bustling with people, so crowded that she couldn't help but brush past some of them as she moved. The area was full of stores. The sound was worse here. It seemed to bounce off the buildings and amplify itself, and Phoenix pushed to get through to the other side.

Once she had crossed, she leaned against the side of the building and tried to control her breathing, which had gotten out of hand.

Veronica wouldn't have been in there, Phoenix reasoned and started walking again.

It seemed no one slept here. Granted, it was still early, but had humans completely forgotten their instinct to be cautious of the night? Humans in Ember knew, even if subconsciously, that vampires were real. The night meant being tucked safe inside, away from all the monsters.

Phoenix supposed that logic didn't make sense anymore since vampires didn't hunt and most other species were more active during the day.

She made her way into a street littered with restaurants whose seating flowed naturally into the open air. Somewhere, a band was playing, the music drifting, but still far enough away that it wasn't overwhelming.

The light was different here. It was still bright enough that the humans could see, but dim enough that the light didn't reach all corners. Long strips of darkness stretched between buildings, and as Phoenix walked down the sidewalk, she realized this was the perfect place for a vampire to feed.

When Phoenix saw the long blonde locks disappearing between a couple of storefronts, she assumed she must be imagining things. She wasn't great at recognizing people, but Veronica frequented the town hall, mostly to complain and cause trouble, and of all the vampires, she was one of the most recognizable. It was why Phoenix had decided that she could take on this job — that and not having a choice in the matter. With no better lead, Phoenix started to run, upsetting a few groups of people congregating on the sidewalks and a few patrons seated in the outdoor dining area.

The alleyway was between a wings shop and a bar, and the scents of spices and alcohol swarmed the area, causing Phoenix to gag involuntarily. She had to focus on the task at hand, so she once again pushed down the sensory stimuli and continued.

When Phoenix turned into the alley, she saw Veronica, her teeth sunk into a young woman's neck. A growl escaped out of Phoenix, causing the vampire to look up.

"You made me spill," she said.

"This isn't funny. You need to come back to Ember with me."

"They sent a puppy after me? They didn't think they could take me themselves?"

"They are preparing for war," Phoenix said. She hoped that since Veronica was talking, it meant they could wrap this up quickly. The vampire would go back, and everything would move forward.

"How exciting." Her hand went to the woman's throat, her fangs ready to sink in again.

"This is serious. You need to return to Ember before everything gets out of hand. The council is dissolving, and more blood will be spilled among your kind."

The gleam went out of Veronica's eyes, and the pretense dropped. "Fine, let me clean up my mess." She leaned down and licked the wound on the woman's neck. There was no fear of her turning into a vampire unless she were kin, but she would have a nasty bruise on her neck with two holes. There was no way around it, but Phoenix was not concerned that anyone would believe her, especially if Veronica came home quietly.

"Go back to work, honey," Veronica told the woman.

"Will I see you again?" the woman asked. Her gaze was disconnected, and her tone was hollow.

"Probably not, but you will do well enough without me."

Phoenix was relatively certain there wasn't anything to the stereotype of vampires' power of suggestion over humans, but the woman seemed to loosen her gaze and perk up as the words were said. A smile returned to her face before she ever left the shadows of the alley, heading to the bar she must have come from due to the scent that covered her.

"So things have gone to shit back home?" Veronica moved seductively toward Phoenix, her hips swaying and her finger twirling around a lock of her hair. Phoenix had never felt even a glimmer of attraction toward anyone, and whatever stunt she was trying to pull was not working.

"No, not yet. But things might get that way if we don't head back soon."

"Well, I guess I still have some work to do."

It was then Phoenix realized that she may not have been seduced, but she was reading the situation completely wrong. Veronica wasn't doing the logical things. She was still intent on whatever she had planned, which wasn't sneaking off to the side of a building for a snack.

"What do you want with all of this? What will any of it serve you?"

Veronica was right next to Phoenix now. She reached out her finger, tracing it along Phoenix's jawline as she spoke. "I want humans to remember the fear of being prey. I want them to remember what it was like to be hunted by us."

Veronica reached up as if to kiss Phoenix, but she stepped back and put her hand in front of Veronica's face to stop it. The vampire stood wide-eyed, seemingly affronted that someone had not fallen for her charms.

"That isn't going to happen," Phoenix said. "This isn't the 1800s. Humans have technology now. They have movies and video games that have made the horror our kind has caused over the years look like a joke. But more than that, they finally have a way of discovering the truth — that there are no greater monsters than what humanity is capable of. They don't need us to haunt them; they do it to themselves."

"I will show them. I will teach them about death before they are reborn in fear!" Veronica screamed. Then she displayed her full fangs, but before Phoenix could react, Veronica was away, running at top speed. Phoenix followed right after, dodging the humans crowding the area, but she couldn't keep up, at least not in her human form.

Phoenix found a dark corner and turned.

Vampires had discovered the science behind why they could turn, but wolves had yet to figure out how they went from a two-hundred-pound human to a creature weighing two-thirds the size. It was less a transformation and more a blinking out of one body and transporting into the next. Within a minute, Phoenix started running on all fours after Veronica's scent.

The transformation always left Phoenix out of sorts. The world was overwhelming as a human, but it was even more so as a wolf. She could hear and smell so much better. Other members of the pack used their forms to their advantage, but Phoenix always felt it put her at more of a disadvantage. She only switched over if there was something the wolf could do better than her human self, like chasing down a vampire.

The trail was still fresh and Phoenix had no problem following it. It led away from all the crowds, taking her toward the housing area where most people were closed up in their houses away from the darkness, not asleep, or at least not always asleep, but settling in. Even still, the sound of the city sunk into Phoenix, even more so running as a wolf.

There was rock music playing in a bedroom, a couple

was arguing, someone was playing a loud video game, and the churning of a blender cut through the night.

And the lights. There would be brief periods of darkness, but then streetlights would highlight an area so bright it might as well have been the sun. Porch lights reached out to the sidewalk. It was as if the people had forgotten what it was like to be in darkness, and Phoenix found she already missed her town.

But she had to stay focused on the hunt. She kept following Veronica's trail. Veronica seemed able to move so much faster than Phoenix. Like their natural counterparts, werewolves could run between thirty to forty miles in their wolf form. And Phoenix, with all her training, was one of the fastest of the pack. Yet she didn't seem to be gaining on Veronica at all, and her stamina was waning. They were made for short runs to take down their prey, not long hunts. Wolves were the epitome of working smarter, not harder, and when Phoenix's legs started giving out on her, she realized that she had lost this round. She shifted back to her human form, and like magic, everything came back. She was dressed in her clothing, and everything was held in her pockets, almost as if her body had been stored somewhere else until she needed it again.

She reached into her pocket and pulled out her phone. Her ability to speak was gone. She could barely drop a pin of her location in a text message to Ancel before she curled up and started rocking on the side of the street right under one of the obnoxiously bright street lights.

Phoenix only knew the police officer had arrived when he touched her, and she let out an involuntary scream at the unanticipated contact. Time had slipped away as everything continued to press down on her, but some part of her mind knew this was not good. She had read the articles and understood the statistics. Her skin, tan from her mother's mixed Latine heritage, was light enough to help protect her. But police weren't trained to understand those in a mental health crisis or the sensory overload Phoenix found herself in.

If shot, she would most likely survive, a privilege her human counterpart couldn't count on. But it would diminish her claims as alpha. She knew she needed to calm down, to pull herself out of this meltdown, but it wasn't that easy. If it had been her choice, she would have never melted down in the first place.

The officer stepped back at her yell and rested his hand on his gun, but he didn't unhook it, a good sign. Phoenix tried to remember her techniques to calm down, but what she needed was a soundproof room and a good nap to recover. Neither of them was imminent. She forced her eyes to focus on the ground in front of her, pulling herself to be more present but also causing herself more long-term damage. Her expression was submissive, and it was hard for Phoenix to pull off when she practiced so hard at being dominant, but it was necessary under the circumstances. The human had to feel no threat from her. This meant she needed to control her movements. No stimming, nothing that would come naturally for her. She had to mask and put the officer at ease when she was the one who needed help, and the unjustness of the world filled her. Phoenix was consumed with the need to fix everything wrong in both the magical and human communities.

But that was beyond her. She needed to focus on what she could protect. Right this second, that was just herself. She brought her breathing under control, consciously trying to even it out and regulate her body. Then, she tried to speak to put the officer at ease, but she wasn't capable of that. Her voice would come back to her eventually, but now it might as well not have ever existed.

The officer was talking to her, but she couldn't make out the words. Sound was just a massive influx overwhelming her auditory processing. He was yelling now, and she knew he wanted her to do something, but she couldn't understand what it was. The tears started falling down her face, unbidden. Alphas didn't cry. She tried to relax her posture to make it more compliant, but her own body was foreign to her, something disconnected from her mind, and the most she could manage to do was to stop the rocking and sudden movements. That took every effort she had. With it came the influx of emotion. There was the frustration at not being able to control her own body, as well as the shame.

There was the anger at always having to perform, to be someone else because who she was was never enough, not for the pack or even here in the human world.

Another howl clawed out of her throat; it was primal, more animalistic than anything a human could produce. The officer took another step back and unsnapped the hook of his gun.

Phoenix heard another car pull up, tires rushing over the asphalt and the sudden squeal of breaks being slammed. Then Ancel was in front of her, not too close and not touching. He brought the familiar scent of the pack and the knowledge that he was hers to protect. But for now, he was the one doing the protecting, standing between the officer and herself. And that knowledge was enough to force her to shove it all further down. She could feel it all sitting inside her, a stone that weighed her down. There had to be healthier options, but she didn't know what else to do.

Einer was talking to the police officer, the words still incomprehensible, but whatever he said seemed to put the officer at ease. Phoenix felt a heavy blanket cover her shoulders. It smelled like a lone wolf — not pack but not human either. The weight helped ground her in the moment, reminding her that her body was her own. With other wolves to protect her, she closed her eyes and let as much of the pain out as possible. The rest she smushed down into the darkness inside of her.

Then she stood up, slowly at first. Ancel stood by her arm, within reach if she should need it but knowing not to touch her. He had seen more of these meltdowns than she would have liked, and out of anyone, he knew how to help. She walked slowly toward the truck's passenger seat and climbed in. Ancel took the driver's seat even though it wasn't his car.

Einer didn't seem to object as he opened the door to the truck's second row of seats and slipped in, despite being bigger and barely fitting in the crunched-up space. With Ancel at the wheel, Phoenix could relax slightly.

As they drove toward the house, Phoenix tried to calm herself but found herself slipping away, dissociating from reality as much as possible. When they arrived, she slipped into her bedroom and closed the door. The silence covered her, and she took her first real breath of the night. She sunk into the softness of the rug, pulling the heavy blanket over her, and went to sleep.

Phoenix slipped her phone out of her pocket where it had been digging into her side. The battery was dead. She found her bag on the bed and shifted her things around until she located her charger. She slipped it into the wall outlet and waited impatiently until it charged enough for the phone to turn on.

There were no missed messages, which meant that her father either trusted her enough to get this job done or that he was communicating with Jared instead. She knew instinctively it was the latter. And maybe he was right. After last night, it was obvious she was in no position to be the pack's alpha. She had lost Veronica on the street. Worse, she had lost herself right there in a subdivision of the city and had almost gotten shot by the police, which would have caused all sorts of problems for the pack to fix.

She checked the time. It was late morning, meaning she had most likely been out for at least ten hours, not too terrible considering how badly she had melted down. Her body always shut down afterward. She stretched her muscles, undoing as much of the clenching as possible. It never went away completely; she held too much stress within herself.

Phoenix did a quick check in her phone's camera. Her hair was in disarray. She reached into her bag to grab her brush and came up empty. She must have forgotten it. Instead, she used her fingers as much as possible to tame down the wild locks.

There were dirt-laden tear streaks covering her cheeks, and all she could hope was to sneak into the bathroom to clean them off before anyone saw. Phoenix stood up, leaving her phone to finish charging, and took a deep breath. She would get through this; she had to get through this. Then she put her hand on the doorknob and opened it. Before she had moved a step toward the bathroom, Jared blocked her way.

"I heard you had quite the night. You should have come with me. I got some excellent leads."

Phoenix tried to push past him, as the words were not ready to start working yet. He just stayed in her way. She growled, low and throaty, the threat real. She looked up at him with all the pent-up anger in full force in her gaze. He lowered his eyes immediately and stepped back, likely before he could even process his reaction. Phoenix moved past him and toward the bathroom. Part of her regretted that he caved so easily. She really needed to hit something. It was the only thing that ended up making her feel like herself.

Instead, she contented herself with getting cleaned up. She considered taking a shower to wash the night completely away, but the thought of the thousands of needles of water hitting her skin was more than she could handle this morning, so she satisfied herself by taking the washcloth and soap and washing herself down vigorously. She wouldn't be as clean, but the deep pressure felt good. She was happy enough with her appearance when she walked out of the bathroom.

Ancel and Einer were already in the living room. Jared was around somewhere. She could smell him, and it was fine with her that he had found a way to make himself scarce for the moment. Phoenix didn't have the patience for his games right now, and she would just as easily rip his head off as try to play them.

"Food," she managed.

Ancel got up and went into the kitchen. Phoenix wasn't sure how long the other wolves had been awake, but none of them had eaten yet, which wasn't abnormal. It would be unusual for an alpha not to eat first. But they either hadn't been up that long or had been unsure how long she would sleep for them to have not even started making breakfast.

Phoenix wasn't particularly hungry, but she also had difficulty recognizing when she needed to eat, and after last night, she would need more food than usual.

Einer disappeared into the kitchen to help cook, a move Phoenix couldn't interpret. He was either there to claim his territory, or he was less dominant and felt the need to provide for her. But some part of Phoenix wondered if he went just because he wanted to. Einer had said he was like her, which meant he also didn't understand all the social games werewolves played. If so, she could see why he would prefer to live all alone, but she couldn't understand his need to be near a city. The city was unsettling, and any wolf that soundproofed their bedrooms had to have the same sensory overload she had.

Phoenix waited until the smells drifted through the

house, and went to the kitchen. Ancel pulled out a chair, and still too tired to do anything, she sat down without thinking. He put a plate in front of her, and she started eating.

Jared walked in, returning from wherever he had been hiding, and grabbed a plate to dish up his own food. Einer slapped his hand down, causing the plate to crash to the floor and shatter.

"This is my house," he growled.

Phoenix tensed, preparing to stand and handle the situation. Jared was her wolf, and she was responsible for his bad manners. Jared looked over at her, flinching at her gaze, and Phoenix wondered what emotions she was allowing to leak through with her tiredness. Then Jared looked back to Einer and decided not to press the issue. He stepped back, allowing the older man to fix his food.

"Clean that up," Einer told Jared.

Jared flinched at the suggestion, probably having intended for Ancel to clean up his mess, as the only non-dominant visiting wolf. Phoenix glared at Jared, letting him know exactly how much she wouldn't stand for that behavior. He had caused the mess, and it had become his responsibility to clean it up.

"The broom and dustpan are in the small cupboard by the fridge," Einer said.

Jared waited long enough to let everyone know he wasn't happy about the situation but not long enough for anyone to step in. Then he went to the tall, skinny door by the fridge and opened it to reveal various cleaning instruments. He reached in, pulled out a broom, grabbed a dustpan from the wall, and returned to the mess.

From the way he awkwardly held the broom, Phoenix

could tell he had never had to clean up after himself before. He would have been better served to have picked up the smaller brush hanging on the wall to make sure all the tiny ceramic pieces were swept off the ground, but he blundered around until he managed to get all the big pieces onto the dustpan before standing up, uncertain what to do next.

"Trash can is under the sink," Einer said between bites.

Phoenix realized she needed to continue eating, or all the placating would be in vain. She continued working on her plate while monitoring the situation, aware that Ancel was standing to the side, waiting for the entire ordeal to end.

Jared dumped the pieces into the trash can and went to put up the broom. The mess wasn't completely taken care of. Phoenix would need to finish the job later when Jared was not around to see, or press the issue now. But before she could move from her seat, Einer shook his head, letting her know he didn't want to force the issue. So she stayed in her chair, pretending to focus on her food.

Seemingly pleased with himself, Jared grabbed a new plate piled with food and sat down to eat.

Only then did Ancel dish up his food, a serving from a meal that he had mostly made, and sat down at the end of the table as far away from the trio as possible.

With their bellies full, they moved into the living room. Phoenix went to sit on the couch but realized that it was one of the soft kinds that allowed you to sink right into the cushions. If anything happened and Phoenix needed to move fast, it would hamper her. However, that didn't stop Ancel or Einer at all. They sat right down.

When Jared stayed standing, Phoenix knew the situation would rapidly deteriorate as each of them competed for dominance. Instead, she walked into the kitchen, pulled out one of the chairs from the table, and brought it back into the living room. Phoenix sat down on it like she didn't have a care in the world.

"Last night, I went to the nightclubs," Jared started speaking. "I couldn't locate Veronica, but I think this is where she will show up. We should all go back, split up, and find her."

"She won't be there," Phoenix said.

"How do you know? You think every plan I make is a failure, but you didn't do any better last night. From what I heard, you had to be rescued and brought back to lick your wounds."

"She won't go to a club because she won't be noticed there. She needs people to see her to get validation, but also to catch her prey. She is planning something that will happen soon and allow her to be seen in a bigger way."

"How could you possibly know that?"

"She all but told me last night."

The room went silent, and Phoenix realized that in her sensory meltdown the night before, she hadn't told anyone that she had found Veronica.

"She was feeding in an outdoor courtyard with restaurants and bars. I caught sight of her and followed her to where she was preying on one of the waiters."

"Then where is she now?" Jared demanded.

"I don't know. She ran, and I chased her. I knew she could run fast, but it was like nothing I had seen before. She never had to stop. I made it to the subdivision where you picked me up, but I don't know if she was running that way to shake me or because she had built herself a safe house out that way."

"You let her get away." Jared slammed his fist on the side of the fireplace, but it was made of pure stone, and he pulled it back with a curse. "If I were there, I would have been able to track her down." He cradled his hand to his chest.

"You weren't there," Einer said. "You decided to storm off without thinking things through. I'm sure you had a fine time dancing and drinking. I doubt you even looked for the vampire, but this is serious. She is hunting in my territory, and she needs to get out before there is a massacre."

Something pulled at Phoenix, something that Veronica

had said to her. She couldn't remember; her brain worked that way sometimes. The more she tried to force it, the harder it was for her to pull out the memories. She had to relax and let it come on its own, but now was not the time for relaxing.

"We need to stake out the area where she was found last night," Jared said. "Vampires are territorial, so she will return to hunt again. She is old, so she must be fed every night."

"Vampires are territorial," Ancel said. "But she is already outside of her territory. She would not have had time to set up a new one in only a few days."

"She wants a show," Phoenix said. "She wants attention and fear. She is blood-mad and won't be thinking rationally. You didn't see her last night. It was like she was thirsting for all the blood and violence, and consequences be damned." Phoenix continued to feel the pull of her words leading her toward what she needed to know, but before she could get there, Jared exploded again.

"She is a vampire. They are all blood-mad. Veronica will go back because she knows it is an easy place to get blood. She outsmarted Phoenix once, so there is nothing that she needs to worry about. What she won't know is that we will all be there."

"Then what?" Ancel asked.

"What do you mean?" Jared asked.

"Then how do we catch her if she shows up? She has already shown Phoenix that she isn't planning on coming home willingly."

"She may not come willingly, but one vampire isn't a match for three werewolves," Jared said. "Once we get her cornered, we should be able to capture her and bring her back without a problem."

"Three werewolves?" Einer asked.

"Me and you two." Jared pointed to the two men. "It seems like it may have been too much for Phoenix, and she may be better off spending the day resting."

Phoenix thought back to the flashing lights and all of the noise. Jared was right; she was too overwhelmed to go back there. If it had been anyone else, they could have kept the presence of mind to have captured Veronica. She had been right there. But Phoenix had not only let her go; she hadn't even managed to follow her.

"Jared is right," Phoenix said.

Ancel and Einer turned and looked at her questioningly.

"I let her go. Things would have turned out differently if I hadn't been so overwhelmed. You tried to warn me, and I didn't listen. You should go with him and stake out the area. We don't have any other leads."

"I think —" Ancel started before Phoenix cut him off.

"I said go." The command left her voice without even thinking about it and Ancel jumped up from the couch and prepared for a night out on the town.

"You made the right call," Jared said.

Phoenix turned to him. "I hope this works. All that matters is that we stop Veronica, and if you can make that happen, then that is what it takes. But you better not cause my wolf any harm."

Jared stepped back from the intensity of her glare but turned and walked away without responding.

"Are you sure this is the best call?" Einer asked.

"No, but I don't know what else to do. I could have ruined everything last night because I wasn't strong enough. She needs to be caught. Who knows how many people she has hurt already."

"So you are trusting things to him?"

"Are you going with them? I understand if it is too much."

"There is a difference between knowing your limits and giving up."

Einer grabbed his jacket and exited through the front door. Jared and Ancel followed shortly after. Phoenix found herself alone in the house. She knew that being with them wouldn't help the situation. She couldn't handle herself last night, but sitting around while others did the work didn't seem right either. She started to pace, checking her phone every few minutes even though there was no way they had even made it into the city.

The trio had to have taken Einer's truck. Ancel's car was probably still parked on the side of the road downtown. There was no way for her to join them at this point, short of picking up the phone and asking for a ride, but she would just distract them.

Phoenix paced some more. As the night wore on and she didn't hear anything, worry began to creep in. Her mind kept arguing between her need to have gone to protect her wolves and the distraction she would have caused. With no word, and no way to release the anxiety, it filled her until she was ready to snap.

The sun was starting to rise before the trio returned to the house. Phoenix was surprised that her pacing hadn't worn a trail into the carpet by the time they arrived.

"What happened?" she asked.

"Nothing happened," Ancel said before sinking down into his makeshift bed at the side of the couch.

"What does that mean?" Phoenix turned toward Jared for answers, but he remained taut.

"We spent the night looking over the area, and there was no sign of Veronica," Einer said. "When it was clear that she wasn't going to make an appearance, we suggested that at least one of us go on recon and scout out some other possible locations, but the commander here wasn't having any of that."

"She will come," Jared said. "We have to return tomorrow and wait for her to show up. She was expecting us tonight, but she won't expect us to be there two nights in a row."

"That is just bad logic," Phoenix said. "We are going to need to come up with another plan. We have to figure out what her next move is. It is there. I just can't figure out what it is."

"Well, while you were here thinking, the rest of us were out doing what needed to be done. Just leave it to us, and we will catch Veronica in no time."

Jared plopped down on the couch and threw his arm over his head. They had been out all night, and Phoenix knew they had to be tired, so she retreated to her room. She started to close the door and was surprised to find that Einer had followed her. He stood in the doorway, not evading her space but making it very clear he wanted to talk.

"Can I come in?"

Phoenix was taken aback by the request. It was his house, but he had gifted the room to her. There was a fine line on whose territory it was, and his asking was a way of skirting the issue. Phoenix stepped back and let him in. He closed the door behind him, and for a brief second, a flash of fear went through her, but she knew she was the tougher of the two.

"I thought it best to have a conversation where we couldn't be overheard."

Phoenix thought about the soundproofing and how it worked both ways, and she became very curious about what he wanted to talk about.

"Do you really think it is best to go along with what that pup thinks? He's not very gifted."

"My father has been grooming him to be the next alpha."

"That is because your father is a great man with very little sense of his own."

Phoenix's jaw fell open. No one inside the pack would dare insult her father that way.

"Maybe if more people had told him, he wouldn't have made some of the decisions that he had, and Ember wouldn't be in the state it is."

Phoenix couldn't help agreeing, but he was outside the pack, and questioning her alpha was not his place. The room seemed to shrink, and Phoenix became aware that Einer was taller than her. She made herself larger and began a low growl.

Einer lowered his gaze slowly to give her dominance but to acknowledge that this was his house. Then he moved to a wooden desk chair and sat down.

"You follow what happens in town?" Phoenix managed to keep her voice even when she spoke.

"I'm not that far away. It is the closest nexus to me, and I am drawn back to it every now and then. It's peaceful, even if navigating pack dynamics is exhausting."

"It is," Phoenix said, able to relax slightly now that dominance had been decided. "I don't know how everyone else can manage it instinctively. They know what to do without trying. I have to think about every single thing. I'm tired."

"So you're giving up?"

"I never said I was giving up."

"Well, it sure seems that way. You're letting Jared direct things, and my city is going to suffer. We will never find Veronica if you keep him in charge."

"I didn't do much better. I lost it in the middle of the city. The police could have shot me. I endangered not just the wolves but the entire magical community. My meltdown could've caused more harm than anything Veronica planned."

"So what?"

"What do you mean?" Phoenix clenched her hands and started beating them softly against her thigh.

"So what? You became overwhelmed by a new situation that was louder than anything you were used to. Of course, it happened. You went out alone without a plan and without backup. The problem is what happened: you thought you had to be perfect, some super alpha who never asked anyone for help. If you had brought backup, maybe we could have found her."

"You didn't want to go. You said it was too loud."

"It is too loud. I think you found that out, but that just meant we needed to figure out the plan, not that we shouldn't have done exactly what you did, just together. Your father said you went to the vampire ranch by yourself. You faced off against the entire pack of them and made a deal that would require him to relinquish his seat. It seems you aren't afraid to upend the system, but remember, you don't have to do it alone."

"You do."

"That's my choice. If you want to be a lone wolf, be my guest. You can set up somewhere down south and stake out your claim. Leave your pack to that imbecile and never look back."

"I can't do that," Phoenix growled.

"Well, you can't have it both ways." Einer kept his eyes trained on the carpet as he spoke. "You either figure out how to be a leader without sacrificing who you are, or you walk away. I walked away, but I didn't have a pack depending on me. It was best for me to walk away. I don't think you would like it all that much, though."

"Why do you think that?"

"Your name. How old were you when you got it?"

"When I was ten. My father thought it best that I wait for the naming ceremony. I didn't talk until a few years before, and he had concerns that our seer would be unable to name me."

"Did they have the same concerns?"

"No."

"And you were named Phoenix. What does that mean?"

"That I am firm, and I have a hot temper."

Einer laughed then. "I guess that is one way of looking at it. Or perhaps, it stands for rebirth — for the pack, for the magical community, but also for yourself. Let go of who you were, and be born into who you are. Being autistic isn't anything bad or to be ashamed of. We just interact with the world differently, and our perspective can give a fresh set of eyes to how things have been done by others in charge."

So that answered it: Einer was autistic. Phoenix had thought so but hadn't considered it polite to ask. Now that he had said it, she realized he had managed to create a life for himself. It was away from the pack, but that worked for him. Phoenix needed her pack. She needed the connection. It grounded her, and she liked to think she grounded them as well. What a unique way of putting it: rebirth of herself, accepting what she had always fought, what she had been told time and time again was bad.

"Wait, rebirth?" Phoenix asked.

"Yes, please tell me I don't have to say it all over again. I don't think I have it in me."

"No, not that at all. I was thinking back to what Veronica said to me. She said that there would need to be death before rebirth. She plans on going to the concert. We need to get everyone up. We need to make a plan. I know where she is headed."

Phoenix was certain they could have found a way to sneak into the Red Rocks Amphitheater. The place was teeming with security, but they were wolves. However, luck was in their favor. They had arrived early and were able to pick up a few general admission tickets when the box office opened. There were a few hours before the amphitheater allowed access for admittance, and Phoenix had them take turns doing as much recon as possible.

Veronica couldn't be out in this direct sunlight, so it was unlikely she was here. However, the wolves needed something to do to help with the anxious energy that came before enacting the plan. They had spent the last two days researching on the computer and listening to Ancel describe the venue, since he was the only one who had visited previously, and they were as ready as they could be.

When the time came, they lined up with the other humans and waited for their turn to enter.

"This had better work," Jared said. "If we missed her big reveal, there won't be time to find her before the deadline."

"If she already had a big reveal, we would know about it," Einer said.

"This is it," Phoenix said. "Everyone just needs to stick to the plan."

When they entered the amphitheater, they came into the center. Below them were assigned ticketed rows. The benches above were general admission, and they stretched up high. Vertigo hit Phoenix as she looked at the rows of identical benches. She turned around and took in where she was. She had grown up in a small town surrounded by the beauty of Colorado, but none of it had prepared her for the walls of red rock encircling her.

"Go take the observation point," Phoenix told Ancel. "If you see anything, text us."

Ancel nodded and headed to the top of the benches. People were entering, and the benches closest to them were filling up. Phoenix walked over to a bench, and when a couple was about to go around them to sit there, she turned and bared her teeth. It was just enough for them to decide they were better off moving somewhere else.

The trio sat down and waited.

As time inched on, more people started to arrive. As they walked past Phoenix, their legs brushed against her own. Behind her, they bumped her as they settled in to find seats. The sound level also increased, the amplification of thousands of voices talking over each other.

The lights turned on as the sun started to drop in the sky. Two large screens spewed white light over the seats, and lights on top of the stage and side of the amphitheater turned on, causing a burst of light to cover the audience.

Phoenix's breathing escalated, and her body began to tense.

"Here. I thought you might find these helpful." Einer handed over a pair of earplugs and over-the-ear protective gear. Phoenix put in the earplugs and then slipped the over-the-ear protection over them. The sound started to turn down, taking the edge off, and Phoenix felt herself relax slightly.

"I didn't think to bring sunglasses," he said.

"This helps. Thank you. I'm sure sunglasses would make me look even more abnormal."

Einar shrugged and put on his own ear protection. He also pointed to a teenager wearing over-the-ear headgear and an adult wearing noise-canceling earbuds. Phoenix spotted still others there who had found their own way of regulating the ambient noise.

"You're not as alone as you think you are. Although most people here don't grow fur."

When the opening band finally started, the sun had set, and Phoenix was sure Veronica was here somewhere. She tried searching the crowd through the flashing lights coming from the stage, but could not see anything.

They had decided that Veronica would most likely wait for the main event, a band called The Zombiez, known for doing elaborate spoofs through their sets. A few years back, they had pushed things too far, making the audience believe that they were partaking in cannibalism on the stage. Venues started canceling them, but they became a cult classic and made their way back. However, they now tended to be more selective about their stunts. They were widely known for eating monkey brains, however. Tonight, the audience might get more than they bargained for, and Phoenix just hoped they would be able to stop Veronica before anything serious happened.

Even with the ear coverings, the music drilled into Phoenix's head. But at least tonight, she had a purpose and a plan. They were in it together.

"We should go now," Jared said. His legs were bouncing in anticipation, and he kept turning as if trying to look everywhere at once.

"It's not time yet," Phoenix said.

Jared let out a low growl. "I'm sick of taking orders from you. I will capture Veronica alone, and the pack will finally be mine." He stood up and stomped off down the row of people toward the stage.

Phoenix half stood up. Einer placed a hand on her shoulder, and she sat back down.

"Your plan is good," he said. "We can pull it off without him."

Phoenix didn't respond. She might not have liked Jared, but he was still hers to protect, and who knew what trouble he was going to get himself in? Right now, her priority was to her whole pack, and to keep them from war, she needed to stop Veronica. So they waited until The Zombiez started tuning up their instruments.

"Ready?" Phoenix asked.

"Ready," Einer said.

Phoenix pulled out her phone and sent a quick text to Ancel.

"It's on."

Then she stood up, headed toward the side, and found the darkest corner she could hide in. Watching for any human attention, she shifted.

The side of the stage was full of security, but they were tuned into human trouble, and Phoenix carefully stayed in the shadows, slinking past them without making a noise.

There was a ramp leading down to the concert's underworkings. Phoenix waited until it was unoccupied and plodded down it. In the tunnels, people were everywhere, busy with the concert that had restarted above. The area under the auditorium was a maze full of hallways, easy to get lost in and never to be seen again. The first few moments were unsettling, the rush of sensory input overloading her. The ear covering had disappeared with her body, and she was left with a rush of noise echoing off the walls. The lights were dim, but the minute flickering of the florescent bulbs pressed into her. The smell of so many bodies in an enclosed space caused her to sneeze. In the intake of breath, she caught Veronica's scent. She put her nose to the ground and followed it, turning through the underground maze. The humans stepped out of her way as if seeing a large dog in their tunnels was an everyday occurrence.

The scent of Veronica was weak at first, but as Phoenix moved, it became stronger. The vampire would not act down here; she would desire a large stage for her production. The hope was that Phoenix could take her down here before any big reveal.

Veronica's scent began to intermingle with Jared's, and Phoenix felt a jolt of fear as she began to follow the wolf's trail. It led into a room with a closed door in a rarely used hallway. The human scents were distant, and more dust hung in the air. Still, Phoenix was cautious as she shifted back into her human form. Certain that no one saw her, she opened the door. The room was small, and enough light from the hallway illuminated the horror inside. Jared was on the floor, his throat half torn out. She rushed to him, slipping in his blood as she reached down to check if he was breathing. Somehow, he was still alive.

"You need to shift," Phoenix said, but Jared was beyond comprehension. She leaned over and opened his eyes, making sure to maintain unblinking eye contact. "Shift"

It was a command that he would not be able to ignore, and Phoenix felt his body begin to change. It was less a shifting of flesh and more a phasing out of one body and the phasing in of another until a wolf was now lying on the ground. Jared's wolf form was whole, but unmoving. Phoenix pictured his body safely tucked away in some pocket universe that allowed for accelerated healing. He would survive, but he wouldn't be conscious for a while.

Phoenix pulled out her cell phone and sent a group chat to Einer and Ancel.

"Change of plans. Veronica hurt Jared. He is unconscious in his wolf form. Ancel, I need you to come help him. Einer, you are now my backup."

Phoenix glanced out the open door, grateful that no one had been around to witness what had happened inside. She shut the door, knowing that there was no way that Ancel would be able to miss the smell of his blood and locate him quickly. Then she shifted back to wolf, the blood going with her human skin until she was a mound of clean brown fur.

At first, Phoenix's nose was full of the scent of blood. It took a few more minutes of wandering before she caught Veronica's scent again. It was too faint, and Phoenix became concerned that she was already too late. She started running, slipping around the humans as they walked. It caused a few more heads to turn, and a few angry shouts, but none of them followed.

Finally, she saw the vampire walking down a hallway

with a tall man in a backward baseball cap and a ginger soul patch on his chin. Phoenix let out a small yip, causing Veronica to turn, a grin filling her face.

"Playtime," she said, grabbing the human and dragging him down another hallway.

Despite popular belief, vampire venom didn't do much more than help a human forget that an event happened. It didn't act as a mood alteration at all, but the man seemed perfectly content to be dragged along by the beautiful woman. His pheromones, or perhaps the help of something external, made him the perfect willing victim.

Phoenix continued after them, doing her best to avoid the humans but never quite able to catch up with Veronica. She followed the scent to the ramp leading out of the tunnel and then slid to a stop. Veronica was walking up the steps to the stage with the man in tow. Phoenix had failed.

Phoenix sprinted the last few feet, but her paws, not made for climbing the steep metal stairs, slowed her down so that by the time she reached the stage, Veronica had already made it past the band and was standing next to the lead singer.

Bright light covered the crowd, making it impossible to see the thousands of people watching the magical community come to life. Phoenix carefully picked her way around the cords, trying to come up with a plan. Veronica was never supposed to have gotten this far, and a werewolf wouldn't be any help, but she couldn't let Veronica expose them all.

Except the band wasn't reacting to them being there. They just kept on playing, and the cheer of the crowd seemed to grow even louder. Phoenix realized that stopping this event might not be the best move. She needed to play it up. So, as Veronica opened her fangs, Phoenix jumped, not to stop her, but like a trained puppy putting on a show. She let out a yip that she knew she would never live down and then went and rubbed up against the singer's leg like she was waiting for a treat.

Veronica had sunk in her teeth and was now feeding on the man who stood contently for the crowd. They were going wild, the cheers so loud that they almost overtook the music.

"Who wants to get sucked tonight?" The singer screamed into the microphone. He paused to let the music overtake the crowd again before continuing. "We are just sheep allowing corporations to suck us dry. We are all undead waiting to be woken up."

The contradiction in the statement seemed lost on the crowd, who started screaming even more.

Veronica stood there, the man still limp at her side. She hadn't even bothered to lick the wound, allowing the blood to seep out the side of his throat.

Phoenix moved from the side of the singer to the vampire. She let her tongue roll out of her mouth in a silly grin that caused the crowd to equally chuckle or sigh in adorableness.

Veronica looked down at Phoenix and let out a hiss. Then she turned to the lead singer and ripped the microphone out of his hand.

"Fear me!" Veronica yelled. "I am the darkness that lingers in the shadow. The nightmare that haunts your dreams. Once, humans ran in fear at the merest sight of my fangs."

Veronica let out a loud hiss into the microphone, allowing the stage lights to reflect off the blood that lingered on their edges.

The crowd was in an uproar, cheering so loudly that

Phoenix couldn't help but flinch at the sound. All their phones were out, with flashes either recording the happening or flickering as pictures were taken. It was more than Phoenix could handle, but she could make out Einer as close to the stage as security would allow him. His face was full of worry, but he held up his thumbs as an awkward show of encouragement. Phoenix let out a yip, followed by another, the tone of "Twinkle, Twinkle, Little Star" amplified by the microphone in Veronica's hand.

Behind them, the drummer laughed, and Veronica turned, grabbing him by the collar of his shirt to maneuver him in front of her. She tilted his neck and opened her mouth.

"Bite him. Bite him." A chant began to echo through the crowd. She sunk her fangs into his neck, and they broke out in applause.

Veronica threw the drummer to the ground and approached the end of the stage.

"Do you not know who I am? I am your death."

The crowd cheered.

Veronica stood frozen as if in confusion. She glanced down to Phoenix and then back to the crowd.

Phoenix looked at Einer and pointed her muzzle toward the stage's stairs.

When Veronica moved toward the lead singer, Phoenix blocked her path, jumping up and licking her face. Veronica grabbed her by the throat and held on to the wolf. A loud boo began to build in the crowd.

"If you want them to hate you, then you will have to kill the wolf in front of them." Einer had made it up to the stage and was now standing to the side of the vampire.

"Those ungrateful humans. How dare they laugh at me. Do they not understand that I am to be feared?"

"That time is long past," Einer said. "Humans cause more harm to themselves and think up more nightmares than we could ever give them. That is why we have had to adapt as a community. I know you want the past to come back, but humans are everywhere, and even if they found out about us, they wouldn't fear us any longer."

The grip around Phoenix's throat loosened, and she dropped to the ground.

"I could take them all. Hunt them down one by one and drain the life out of them. That would make them scared." Her eyes bulged, and she stuck out her fangs and hissed at the crowd. Little spittles of blood flew from her mouth. The crowd cheered again.

"What do you want from all this?" Einer asked.

The drummer had made his way back to his seat and had begun a new song. He was joined by a guitarist, and soon, the rest of the band and the lead singer started playing. They were forgotten on the stage as the crowd started to join in with lyrics that Phoenix couldn't discern as words. The sound thrummed in her head, and all she could think about was getting away, yet somehow, she still managed to hear when Veronica spoke.

"I just wanted to feel alive again."

Einer grabbed Veronica's arm and guided her to the edge of the stage. Phoenix followed behind them.

A small group of stagehands was waiting at the end of the stairs.

"That was epic. The fans will be talking about that for years," one said.

"Who arranged all this?" a woman with a black bob and

pursed red lips asked. She held a clipboard and had an earpiece in one of her ears. She seemed to be in charge. "Someone should have run this by me. Where is the animal handler? We must make sure that we are following proper protocol after what happened in Houston."

Phoenix looked at Einer to make sure he had control over Veronica before she darted under the stage. She passed all the people working on electronic equipment until she found a corner encased in shadows. She shifted back to human form and slipped out before anyone noticed.

Einer and Veronica were right where she left them, still standing by a group of humans who were either congratulating Veronica on such a great performance or questioning her about who had set the whole situation up. Phoenix slid up to her side.

"Let's go," she said, grabbing her free arm. They both kept a firm grip on Veronica as they walked down the ramp and back to the underground tunnels.

Ancel was waiting in the room with Jared, who was still asleep. When he saw Veronica, he backed up further in the room, away from the vampire. Veronica let out a hiss, causing Ancel to jump.

"Enough," Phoenix said. She tightened her hold and opened the door to the room next to where Jared was. It looked unused, with some empty crates littered around the floor.

"Ancel, I need you to clean out the room."

It only took him a few minutes to move the crates to another room before he returned to tending Jared. Einer and Phoenix escorted the vampire in.

"I need to make a phone call," Phoenix said.

Phoenix left Einer in the room with the vampire, stepping out into the hall. Everyone would hear everything, but sometimes, the illusion of separation was more important than actual separation. She selected the number from her phone, which picked up on the first ring.

"We need one of your vans. I'll text you the address."

They stayed stuck in the tunnels until most of the humans had left. Veronica had tested the wolves through the evening with bouts of snarling and attempts to run past. But Vampires hated the taste of wolves. Once Ancel overcame his initial fright, he helped stand guard, and the three kept her contained.

The sun was still an hour from rising when Phoenix felt her phone vibrate, letting her know Veronica's ride was here.

"Stay here and guard Jared," Phoenix told Ancel. Then Phoenix and Einer each held one of Veronica's arms firmly. She thrashed and pulled as they walked down the empty corridors, but the wolves refused to let her out of their grasp.

"Enough!" The shrill voice echoed down the hall, and Veronica froze at the sound. "You may let her go."

"Vampire Mistress." Phoenix gave a nod of respect.

"So formal, young one. Call me Elizabeth."

Elizabeth was dressed casually in jeans and a navy shirt.

She looked young, around eight years old, but she had led the vampires for longer than Phoenix had been alive.

Phoenix let go of Veronica and directed Einer to do the same. Two vampires Phoenix didn't recognize surrounded Veronica and began to lead her down the hall. Veronica snapped at one of them, but when Elizabeth let out a low hiss, any signs of aggression disappeared.

"I didn't expect you to come personally," Phoenix said.

"You cleaned up our mess. It seemed fitting that I should come and thank you myself."

"I wonder why the vampires needed the wolves to solve their problem," Einer said.

Elizabeth turned her attention toward the wolf as if noticing him for the first time. She started walking around him, slowly, as if taking all of him in.

"Tall, dark, and handsome. You are just my type." She practically purred as she spoke.

"I, um, I," Einer sputtered. "No offense, Mistress, but you are not my type."

The old vampire let out a long sigh. "It is probably better that way. I used to eat people who thought otherwise."

"You didn't answer my question." Einer stared down at the vampire, and Phoenix became concerned that he had pushed things too far, but the trio waited in tense silence until Elizabeth responded.

"Ember is not what it once was. I would have chased down my lost sheep, but when the next alpha of the werewolves showed up on my doorstep and offered to do it for me, well, it was an opportunity I couldn't turn down."

"An opportunity?" Phoenix asked.

"Yes. It was a chance for me to see exactly what kind of wolf you are."

Phoenix clasped her jaw shut to stop herself from spurting out the obvious question. She wanted to know what the vampire thought about whether they could work together, but an alpha took charge.

"Whatever your reason, the deal was struck," Phoenix said. "Veronica has been returned to you, and my father has agreed to step down from the council. Will there be peace again in Ember?"

"We will find out, young one. I will see you when night falls again on your territory. I should go now before I burn."

Elizabeth flashed them a sweet smile that sent shivers down her spine, and then she turned and disappeared down the tunnel.

"I'm glad there are no vampires in the city," Einer said.

"I don't know. It seems like you may have a secret admirer."

Einer's eyes widened in pure horror and Phoenix didn't stop the laughter that escaped out of her.

"Let's go get the pups," Phoenix said when she stopped laughing. "It's time for us to head home."

Phoenix faced Einer outside of his home. Now that it was time for them to leave, she realized how hard it was to say goodbye. Even though they had been here less than a week, the time had changed her.

"Goodbye. Thank you for everything," Phoenix said.

They stood awkwardly by each other. Einer had his hands stuffed in his pockets. Phoenix had hers tapping easily at her side.

"You should come again. I told Ancel he could stop by the next time he came to town for one of his concerts."

"He would like that. Maybe I will come along if I can get away."

"If things don't go your way, you can stay until you can get on your feet."

Phoenix looked over at Jared in the back of the car. He had woken up an hour ago and shifted back to his human form. Due to the wolves' magic, there wasn't even a scar where Veronica had attacked him just the night before.

"I don't plan on taking you up on that offer. I am glad

being a lone wolf works for you, but I need my pack, and they need me."

"Jared is a lot like your father when he was younger. I don't mean his lack of common sense, although a bit of that as well. He was rash when he was younger and always thought his way was correct. Maybe if I had stayed and forced a place in the pack, it wouldn't have been as hard for you."

"My only regret," Phoenix said, "is that he didn't introduce me to you sooner. Thank you for helping me see that I don't always have to do things my father's way."

Einer gave her a slight nod as she moved to the passenger's seat. Ancel loaded all three of the wolves' bags into the trunk and took his place in the driver's seat.

Jared had sat up and spread his legs out to take up as much space as possible. He leaned back, ignoring the other two wolves as if he were expecting to be chauffeured home like a hero.

The drive back was quiet. Phoenix expected Jared to try to assert dominance, but instead, he just closed his eyes and went to sleep. Some part of Phoenix hoped that his vocal cords had not survived the vampire attack.

About halfway home, Phoenix got a ping on her phone and was surprised to see that Elizabeth had sent a video. It was a recording of the night before that, judging from the bouncing filming, had been captured by an audience member's phone.

Phoenix suspected there would be minimal repercussions for Veronica's outburst. It had ultimately been a much-needed holiday for the vampires, and in the end, there was not even a loss of human life. That is about as successful as a blood-lust could be. The fact that it got the vampires to head the council would make it much sweeter. At most, Veronica would be confined to the Ranch for a decade. Hopefully, in that time, she would find something to occupy her attention. Acting seemed like a good hobby. Maybe she could become a content creator.

By the time they had made it back to Ember, she was stiff and ready for her own space. The noise from the concert still echoed in her head, and her body had not been able to relax even after they had handed Veronica over. All she wanted was a hot shower and a nap before that night's meeting.

When they pulled in front of the pack house, Jared launched him out of the car as soon as Ancel stepped off the brakes. He didn't even wait for the ignition to turn off.

"This can't be great," Phoenix said.

"There is no way your dad can deny you did this without him, can he?"

"I think my dad may have stopped seeing what was happening with the pack years ago." It hurt Phoenix to say those words. She loved her father more than anything but could no longer deny this simple fact.

"Do you still think he will name Jared his heir?"

Phoenix stepped out of the car, lifting her arms to stretch out all the kinks. "I don't know. I do know that I will do everything I can to stop it from happening."

By the time Phoenix had made it into the house, Jared had her father cornered.

"It's done," Jared said. "I have saved the pack."

Ancel walked in right behind Phoenix, and upon hearing the words, he dropped all the bags he was carrying and started to rush to set the record straight. But Phoenix put a hand on his chest, keeping him back. She shook her head and placed herself against the wall, crossing her arms and waiting.

"Veronica is back with the bloodsuckers, and I have shown that I have what it takes to be alpha."

"Veronica was returned to the vampires last night," Phoenix said. "You were recovering from having your throat torn open because you disobeyed orders. You had no part in her capture except to get in the way."

"You were hurt?" her father asked.

"I'm fine. It was nothing. Being an alpha is about defending your pack," Jared said.

Phoenix couldn't help but roll her eyes. Jared only defended himself. She moved between the two men to get her father's attention.

"The Vampire Mistress will be coming to the pack house tonight to discuss the end of the war and your stepping down from the council."

"What right do they have to ask anything of us?" Jared asked. "We cleaned up their mess for them. They should be grateful."

"Enough," the alpha said. "Well done. You have stopped a war and should be very proud of yourself."

Despite everything, her father was still looking at Jared when he spoke.

"*I* stopped a war," Phoenix said. "I did it with the help of Ancel and the lone wolf. Jared just got in the way. You two pups go home and get some rest."

She couldn't help the satisfaction she felt seeing Jared obey her as he and Ancel walked out the door. She turned to her father. "Do you need any help with the preparations for tonight?"

"No, no. I've got it." He waved her off as he headed toward his office.

Phoenix grabbed her bags and went upstairs.

Phoenix had managed a shower and a few hours of sleep before she left her bedroom and headed into the meeting room. The room was on the bottom floor on the side of the house, so it had its own entrance. It was large enough for an oval conference table and a counter for receiving refreshments. She had expected to be met with the scent of pack and cleaning solution in preparation for the vampire delegation. Instead, the room had remained closed since it was last used. Judging from the stale scent of old donuts, it had probably been for some pack business.

She should have forgone sleep and been down here to handle the arrangements herself, but her father had told her that he would. The sun was going down, and the vampires could show up at any moment. The room was far from ready.

Phoenix had only managed to make some minor adjustments before the sun had completely disappeared, and a knock sounded on the side door. She opened it and looked down to see the Vampire Mistress.

"The brave wild wolf greets us," Elizabeth said.

"Vampire Mistress," Phoenix said before stepping aside to allow entrance.

Behind her, there were two vampires. The first had been changed when he was older. He stood with a scowl, like he would rather be anywhere but where he was at that moment. Yet the lines seemed to have set in, and Phoenix suspected that it was a regular expression. She had not seen him before, which made her wonder at his inclusion.

The other vampire was Veronica. She stood poised in a red dress that would have been more fitting at a ball than a meeting. She smiled in greeting, looking almost nothing like the blood-mad women that Phoenix had encountered less than a day prior. Phoenix stared at the woman for what she knew to be an inappropriate amount of time. Her mind couldn't make the connection to how she could have pulled herself together so quickly and why she was now inside pack headquarters. Phoenix realized the vampires were now waiting on her, and she went into host mode.

"Vampire Mistress, your seat."

The vampire stepped forward, took one look at the chair, and raised an eyebrow at the wolf.

"It had recently been pointed out to me that my differences do not make me weak; they are a part of who I am. I would not wish to use someone else's differences against them in an attempt to gain an upper hand."

The vampire gave a smirk that Phoenix could not interpret and then climbed into the chair that Phoenix had pulled out of storage. It had been specially made with rungs that allowed the shorter vampire to climb onto a raised platform, putting her on an equal footing with the rest of the adult-formed bodies when seated. Once she was settled, the older vampire pushed her in and sat in the chair beside her. Veronica followed, flowing smoothly over the floor despite the three-inch red heels that enveloped her feet. She waited at the edge of the chair, making a slight sound in the back of her throat. The male vampire rolled his eyes and started mumbling nonsense, but he stood up and pulled out her chair, helping push it back in once she was seated. Then he sat back down.

Vampires had their own politics, ones that Phoenix had been studying since she was a pup. The man possessed more power, since he sat beside the vampire mistress. Yet, he was younger than Veronica, or he would not have given in to her whims to be treated with extra respect. It meant that Veronica might not have been an outcast, but she had been punished for her actions. Phoenix had been concerned when she had seen the woman allowed outside of the Ranch, but the interaction had put her fears to rest.

Her father had to have heard the guests' arrival, yet he had still not shown up, so Phoenix excused herself and went to locate him. She found him in his study, sitting behind his solid oak desk. Jared was in a seat in front of him, in the same chair Phoenix normally used.

"The vampires have arrived. They are awaiting your presence." Phoenix didn't hide the annoyance from her voice at having to come and collect him, but like usual, he didn't seem to sense it. Instead, he looked at her in confusion. "They are the delegation I told you would arrive to discuss the conclusion of the agreement you approved." For the first time, Phoenix wondered if it wasn't just his alpha nature that was causing his behavior, but something else, something that she needed to be more watchful of. She had never heard of a wolf having dementia, but she couldn't help but wonder if her father might need to get checked out.

"Oh right, see them in," the alpha said.

"They are already seated and waiting in the meeting room."

Phoenix turned and started walking back. She was relieved to hear the sounds of her father rising and following her. Jared's footsteps came after his.

"Perhaps it would be better if Jared waited in your office," Phoenix said.

"Nonsense. He needs to be here for this."

Phoenix turned to him and let out a low growl, causing Jared to take a step back. Satisfied, Phoenix continued after her father.

Once Phoenix was back in the room, she paused for a fraction of a second, uncertain where to sit. Then she pulled out a chair and sat down opposite the older vampire. When her father entered the room, she did not bother to get up, a disrespect that she would never have done before, but she was too upset at Jared's inclusion to care. The vampire mistress seemed to notice the choice, but it seemed not to faze her father in the slightest, another sign that caused her worry. If she had done something so disrespectful when she was younger, he would have never let it go unchallenged.

Instead, he just sat down like nothing was wrong.

Jared shot her a glare before he sunk into the third seat opposite Veronica.

"Welcome to my house," the alpha said. "To what do I owe the unexpected visit?"

If the welcome was startling, the vampire didn't let it show. Elizabeth continued as smoothly as if her father had given her an appropriate greeting. "We are here to make sure the agreement goes into effect."

"And what agreement are you referring to?"

"The one where you agree to step down from the council to stop the war."

"It seems you should be thanking us for cleaning up your mess. Your vampire went rogue, and it took my wolves to get her back before things went out of control. You should be hoping that we stay in control for another decade."

"What are you saying?" Phoenix asked.

"I have been talking with Jared, and he will be named my heir and moved to the head of the council in my stead. Given his role in helping to save your vampires, this should be something you should welcome. You will not go to war, because you know your vampires will not last against my wolves. It took ours to control your own."

"What is this?" Phoenix smacked her hand down on the table and stood up, facing her father.

"It's alright, young one." The grin that spread across the Vampire Mistress's face sent a shiver of fear down Phoenix, though she tried not to let it show. "We know that your father has been having difficulties lately. So we will talk, for now."

Phoenix sat down but remained on the edge of her seat, her body tense, ready for action, even if she didn't know what that action would be. She found herself siding with the vampires over her own pack. It was unsettling.

"You plan to put this spoiled child on as head of the council?" Elizabeth asked. "I can guarantee that if you do so, no one will stand by you. He had no part in helping to bring one of our lost back into the fold. I have brought Veronica to testify."

"It was Phoenix who led the pack," Veronica said. She glanced at the Vampire Mistress, giving a slight scowl before continuing in an unnaturally sweet voice. "She helped to contain the situation with her quick thinking and ultimately convinced me that it was in my best interest to return to my kind. She also somehow withstood my considerable charms even when they were at their best. She kept the humans safe until my ride arrived. This pup wasn't even a good snack. I still can't get the taste of his blood out of my mouth."

"You can't possibly believe a bloodsucker over me," Jared said.

"There is video," Phoenix said.

The man pulled out a cell phone and grunted at it a few times as he pushed some buttons until a video started to appear. The sudden loud music startled Phoenix, causing her hands to cover her ears, even though it did little to minimize the noise. He thankfully reduced the volume of the phone to one of its lowest settings before handing it over to her father. He watched. Phoenix heard the music looping repeatedly as different views showed the same situation. She couldn't even begin to imagine what he could be thinking as he watched her in wolf form on the stage.

"This fixed the situation?" he finally asked.

"The concertgoers thought it was part of the show. Phoenix pulled herself off as a trained dog, and Veronica came across as special effects. Some comments even criticized them as bad special effects. The humans did not believe it was real, and there was no harm to the magical community. It was all thanks to your daughter's quick thinking."

"Where were you?" The alpha had turned to Jared.

"You told me to make sure she stayed safe. Her plan was ridiculous, so I went to handle the situation on my own."

Veronica let out a long, lyrical laugh. "The poor pup was infatuated with me in less than a second. It was too easy. I didn't even bother playing with him before I ripped out his throat. I guess I should have stayed a little longer to make sure he didn't survive."

Jared stood up and growled at Veronica.

"Want to go again, little wolf? Do you think you could make it more entertaining this time?"

"Enough," the alpha ordered.

Jared sat back down in his chair, scowling at Veronica.

"The vampires cannot afford to be aligned with weakness," Elizabeth said. "You need to fix your pack."

"You did all this?" Phoenix's father asked as he turned to her.

"Yes," she said.

"I have much to think about. I will call a council meeting for tomorrow night." He stood up and started to walk away. Jared stood too, as if to follow him, but the alpha turned back to him. "You will go to your home and not leave until I have told you otherwise." Then he disappeared in the direction of his office.

Jared stared at Phoenix with open hatred but left the house.

"Thank you," Phoenix said.

"You brought our sibling home. You worked to keep us

away from war. You will be a good alpha. All we can hope is that your father comes to his senses."

"What if he doesn't?"

"Then I guess my vampires will get their war after all."

The man stood up and pulled out the Vampire Mistress's chair, waiting until she had climbed down before pulling out Veronica's chair. Then they turned. The two vampires may have been twice as tall, but it was evident that the young vampire held real power and respect. Once they had walked out the door, Phoenix slunk back down in the chair and allowed her body to go limp.

Phoenix hadn't seen her father all day. He kept himself shut up in his office, and when Ancel came to pick up Phoenix for the meeting, his office door remained fully shut. Unsure what else to do, they left and headed toward the council room.

The room seemed more crowded than normal, and Phoenix was glad to have her noise-canceling headphones firmly on her head.

It seemed nearly every species was in attendance, even those without seats on the council. There were the nymphs, the witches, and the vampires, of course. But there were visitors that hadn't made it into the town of Ember itself for a few years. Phoenix found herself surprised to see an elf outside of their forest. Then, the new bartender was there as well, representing the selkie. Phoenix wondered what his story was, how he had ended up as Rocko's newest adopted kin. The closest family of selkies were on the northwest coast.

By the time Phoenix's father arrived, the room was packed, and Phoenix had to edge her way into the middle of the pack to keep from touching strangers. She was surprised when Jared did not arrive with her father, but she found him on the opposite side of the stage, huddled with his group of friends. His face was twisted in rage, and Phoenix felt a kinship with him. Neither knew exactly what the alpha would do and who would be losing their pack.

The room started to fall silent as the alpha made his way from the door to the stage, the crowd automatically making way for him. Phoenix watched as he went up the three steps to the raised platform. It had been a while since he was not the first one present, a while since she had watched him make sudden movements, and she realized how old he had gotten. Once, he would have leapt over those steps, and now he walked up them slowly. It wouldn't mean much to most of those in the room, but for the wolves, he had just broadcasted his age. He left himself with no choice but to name an heir today or open the pack up to be taken by someone stronger.

Her father went to the podium. The room instantly silenced, the bodies so still that no movement could be heard. He paused as if battling within himself, not wanting to say the words but knowing, finally, that they needed to be said.

"Thank you all for coming. As you know, I am due to step down as leader of the council. Per the articles of the pact created centuries ago, the next decade will be overseen by the vampires. Tonight, I will be handing over the head of the council to whomever they delegate as their representative."

There was a collective gasp in the room, and whispers started up, albeit carefully, as almost everyone in the room could hear them. Yet, Phoenix knew that this was the least important thing that her father had to do today, at least in his opinion. That is why he had led with this news. Phoenix wasn't sure if he had predicted the uproar it would cause, but he waited patiently until people realized he was not finished, and the conversations eventually fell silent again.

"As many of you are aware, I have not yet selected the heir to our pack. I will do so tonight."

Even though Phoenix knew it was coming, it still overwhelmed her. She was not ready to leave her pack behind. Although she had prepared, just in case. She had a small pack in Ancel's car. It was all she would have to take with her if she was cast out from the pack for being a second son. Even though she was firstborn. Even though she had shown that she was capable of protecting her people. She inched back against the wall, closer to the other species and farther away from her own. She knew the other wolves sensed what she was doing, and if they weren't in a room surrounded by the entire magical community, they might have acted on the desire to tear her apart. It wasn't personal. It would come with the need to ensure the pack remained strong.

Ancel, her ever-faithful friend, put himself between her and the pack, knowing they would not strike him down, not even after he disbanded from the pack to join Phoenix. She felt a pang of regret that her friend would do that for her, that he would leave it behind to make sure that she wasn't left alone. It was more than him not finding a place here without her; it was a true pack bond.

Phoenix almost didn't hear the words her father said next. It was only when Ancel poked her in the ribs to get her attention that she started focusing back on the moment.

"Parents are not perfect, as those of you who have children know. We try to do what is best for our people, and we try to do what is best for our offspring. But I have recently learned that often it is those who are coming into their own who tell us how we need to proceed. We need to be open to listening. My heir has shown themself to be courageous, adaptable, and, most importantly, to work toward not only the pack's needs but the magical community's needs. They are why we are standing here today at peace, and not meeting tomorrow as enemies. I am pleased to announce Phoenix as the rightful heir to the pack, and I only hope she forgives me for waiting so long."

The words didn't sink in at first. She was so afraid of being hurt that the first thing that made it real was Jared's scream. He let out a long string of expletives that left most of the room in shock and a few individuals impressed. But that was when it sunk in that he would have to leave; by vying for the heir and losing, he had put himself in the position of the second son. He would need to leave the pack or be killed. It was now Phoenix's job to enforce this.

She stepped up, the room parting for her as it had done for her father. She thought about taking off her headphones but decided it was better that they got used to her like this, to know that she could still lead even while utilizing modifications that helped her interact with the world.

"Jared, you have been exiled from the pack. You will leave now and never come back. If you are seen within a hundred miles of the pack, your life will be mine."

He jumped at her, but Phoenix held firm. She had anticipated that exact reaction. His friends held him back, but part of Phoenix wanted him to attack. She would no longer have to hold back, and she would enjoy the fight, no matter how short it lasted.

Jared must have seen the hunger on her face because he stopped pressing forward and now only stood there as a matter of show.

Phoenix turned to his group and addressed them. "Go, take him out of our territory. Join him if you wish, or stay if that is your desire. Just remember that he is no longer pack."

Some tension eased in the group, and one of his friends grabbed his arm and dragged him toward the door. Jared had already stopped putting up a fight. Phoenix knew that a lot of times, everyone was exiled when they ran together in a tight group, like he had. However, Phoenix also knew that the group was not very loyal to Jared. They followed him because they felt they had to. Now, she had given them a choice, and they would have to live with whatever they decided.

The rest of the council progressed without incident. Her father gave up his position to the Vampire Mistress, as expected. However, for one brief moment, she was concerned that Veronica would be appointed instead. After all, the woman had once more been let out of the Ranch. Phoenix was staring at the back of her head, her long blonde hair perfect once again. She seemed to be talking to the witch council member like it was any ordinary day, and not as if a few days ago, she had plotted to upend everything. Phoenix had heard blood-lust could come and leave suddenly, but this she didn't trust.

Phoenix sensed people stopping too close to her. They were not wolves. Phoenix smelled the forest on them and knew that two Nymphs were now behind her.

"That is about time. It will be our turn next, but at least a woman is leading the council," the older nymph said.

The younger one stood in silence, seeming to know that her contribution was unnecessary as her mother extolled the virtues of female leadership.

Suddenly, there was a bump, and the younger nymph's body pushed into her own. Phoenix tried to step away from the people, but the room was still crowded, and as heir, she would need to stay until all the other wolves left, including her father.

"I'm sorry. I'm not sure how that happened. Everyone seems to be overly excited today." Phoenix had heard the voice before. He was one of the male vampires, although she couldn't remember his name. Phoenix looked up to see if she needed to respond and realized he wasn't talking to her at all, but to the nymphs.

"Oh, I think I know you. My partner, Lucas, met you out by the river."

"I think you must be mistaken," the younger nymph finally said.

"Do you mean the one who chose to be a man?" the older nymph asked.

"Now, hey, no need to talk like that. He didn't choose anything except to be who he is. I think you may understand a thing or two about that."

"What do you mean by that?" the older nymph asked. "What do you *mean* by that?"

"I think I made a mistake. I'm so sorry. I was just putting my foot in my mouth; it is kind of my thing. Don't worry about anything I said." His tone became formal. "Ma'am," he said. Then it turned more casual again, "Birk, if you ever need anything, just let Lucas and me know."

Then he was off, but even Phoenix could feel the anger

vibrating off of the older nymph. "What term of respect is Birk, and why would you ever need a vampire's help?"

"Birk is … well … it is my name … that I use … sometimes."

"And why would you think that you needed a new name?"

The mother seemed to pull the daughter out of the council meeting, but Phoenix was unable to hear them anymore.

The room was emptying out now. Most of the wolves had left and her father was on the way out. Ancel waited patiently by the side wall, a huge grin on his face. Phoenix couldn't help but return it. They had done it.

ACKNOWLEDGMENTS

Writing an acknowledgment page is always bittersweet. I have spent so much time with these characters and am now sending them out into the world for you all to meet. Phoenix was such an amazing book to write. I was thrilled to be back with an autistic main character, but it also was the first sequel that I have ever written. I thought it would be hard, and it was in all the ways that writing a book is hard work. However, I have fallen in love with the town of Ember. There are so many more characters that I want you to meet. I finally understand how authors can have sixteen or more books in a series.

Of course, I couldn't have made this book what it was without the community around me. Xel has listened to me go on about my characters for countless hours and sits patiently while I work out details of the book, even though they would rather be doing anything else. AJ is always available to talk about anything when I need a break from writing. Lillian, Anne, and Tessy who were amazing Beta readers. Phoenix would not be what it is today without their feedback - both what worked and didn't work.

I am so thrilled to have continued working with my amazing editor, Rebecca Scharpf. I appreciate the love and polish you give my characters. Editing may not be easy, but it is better with your notes. To Skye Alley for proofreading and polishing this book before it goes out to the readers, as well as giving a voice to them. This is my fifth book and the fifth one that she has narrated. Here is to working together for many more!

And a huge thank you to you, reader! We cannot do this without your support. It is even so much more appreciated as an indie author. Thank you for sharing my books, leaving reviews, and falling in love with my worlds as much as I have. My goal is to bring queer and neurodiversity into fiction. I hope I have done this for you.